PRAISE FOR IT'S ONLY TEMPORARY

"Eric Shapiro's *It's Only Temporary* is an apocalyptic masterpiece: harrowing, hilarious, disturbing, heartfelt, and suspenseful. Not to be missed!"
—James Rollins, best-selling author of *Sandstorm*

"*It's Only Temporary* reads like a road movie travelling toward Armageddon, and its powerful, stylish writing and raw emotion will stay with you for a long, long time."
—Tim Lebbon, Bram Stoker Award-winning author of *Desolation*

"Eric Shapiro has created a gloriously horrific, touchingly intimate tale of the surreal reality of a world turned inside out; of one man's very human, very brutal struggle to 'grow the fuck up' as everything around him races headlong into madness."
—Elizabeth Massie, Bram Stoker Award-winning author of *Sineater*

"Relentless. Shapiro delivers a compelling narrative."
—Jack McDevitt, Darrell Award-winning author of *Eternity Road*

"Shapiro has crafted a damn near perfect Apocalypse story in *It's Only Temporary*; it shuns the usual trappings of the genre, concentrating on people and life rather than impossible schemes and crazy gadgets. A very engaging read!"
—Michael Oliveri, Bram Stoker Award-winning author of *Deadliest of the Species*

Turn the page for more praise...

S0-BBJ-216

"Eric Shapiro has produced a manic road-trip story set at the edge of both the end of the world and his narrator's sanity. In spite of the energetic, farcical feel of the book, *It's Only Temporary* delineates eerily the all too credible behavior that could occur in extreme circumstances."

—Neil Ayres, author of *Nicolo's Gifts*

"A sweet tale wrapped in acid. Virtuoso storytelling, a wonderful blend of optimism and nihilism. Fierce and addictive, *It's Only Temporary* will stay with you a long, long time."

—Adam Connell, author of *Counterfeit Kings*

"This is a strange book for sure, but—if you're feeling strange—you'll find *It's Only Temporary* gripping and worthwhile. The apocalyptic tension builds to a climax that's equally surreal and realistic, while the characters' reactions in the face of death are chillingly believable."

—Marty Beckerman, author of *Generation S.L.U.T.*

"Shapiro takes us on a riveting journey—a poignant coming of age story for a young man deprived of his future. Shapiro's writing is smart, funny, and refreshingly honest. *It's Only Temporary* is both a page-turning adventure and a thoughtful meditation on our existence."

—Peter Buchman, screenwriter of *Eragon*

"I read *It's Only Temporary* in one fast sitting—it's the kind of slangy, stinging, pedal-to-the-metal stuff nobody does anymore—[Shapiro] could revive the entire Impending Doom genre—cool!"

—Christopher Fowler, author of *Full Dark House*

"Sarcastic, wisecracking, reckless yet lovable fool, check. Old school rock soundtrack, check. This is a GOOD thing. I found this utterly refreshing, and the writer knows exactly how to deliver the punchlines."
—Miss Nailer, Headpress

"Eric Shapiro is here—keep an eye out. [*It's Only Temporary*] resonates with horror, dread, and—rarest of all—genuine emotion. And more. The intense emotional drive of *It's Only Temporary* assures me that Eric Shapiro is here to stay, no matter how much he disturbs us."
—William J. Grabowski, author of *The Untold*

"*It's Only Temporary*—a wild ride through the last few hours of a young man's life—will kick your adrenal glands into high gear."
—Michael Bracken, author of *All White Girls*

"The end of the world has been done before but no one has done it quite the same as Shapiro. This story is insane, yet believable. His characters are perfectly pitched against a palpable background of hysteria. I felt compelled to read this as though I had to finish it before the meteor hit. Absorbing stuff."
—Andrew Hook, author of *Moon Beaver*

"[*It's Only Temporary*] will make you feel as insane and adrenalin-rushed as the speedy momentum this story thrives on. Eric Shapiro writes with a fervor and style that makes for true brazen storytelling with a strong sense of how the mind—in a state of utter panic—works."
—Nancy Jackson, editor of *Mind Scraps*

ALSO BY ERIC SHAPIRO

Short of a Picnic

IT'S ONLY TEMPORARY

Eric Shapiro

Edited by D.L. Snell

Permuted Press
www.permutedpress.com
Mena, AR, USA

A Permuted Press book / published by arrangement with the author

ISBN: 0-9765559-3-X

It's Only Temporary © 2005 by Eric Shapiro.
Cover art © 2005 by Ian Jarvis.
All rights reserved.

Without limiting the rights under copyright reserved above, no part of this publication may be reproduced, stored, or introduced into a retrieval system, or transmitted, in any form, or by any means (electronic, mechanical, photocopying, recording, or otherwise), without the prior written permission of both copyright owner and the above publisher of this book.

Visit Permuted Press online at http://www.permutedpress.com

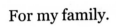

For my family.

1.

"So, what're you gonna do now?"

That's *the* question, isn't it? That's the only question we have. All the other questions are supporting players to that one. You can ask yourself if you paid the rent last month, ask yourself if you should leave your husband, ask yourself if you're in the mood for pasta, but when you boil it all down, you're left with:

"What now?"

On this day, the question is particularly hard. Perhaps *excruciating* is a better word. There won't be other days for doing other things. This, as they say, is it. Whatever you do, you had better choose wisely, and you had better do it right. Or wrong. It really doesn't matter in the grand scheme of things. Because pretty soon, there will be no grand scheme of things.

Tonight, just before seven in my time zone, the clouds will part and the sky will darken and a giant rock—far too giant for words—will enter the ocean and pound the earth, just off the coast of New Zealand, turning us all into God-knows-what (assuming, of course, that there is a God; most of us have been wondering about that lately). This rock will hit the planet so hard that no matter where you're standing, no matter what closet you're hiding in, no matter how sturdy the foundation of your home is, you will fall (or if you're lying down, shake) so violently that your bones will shatter and your life will end. The same goes for most of your worldly possessions. The same goes for all animals. (Many bugs, however, will be spared.) The orb will go silent. Your body will eventually deteriorate. Your checkbooks and foodstuffs and music collection (all of them dusty and broken) will be available for the scrutiny of any aliens that may eventually pass through. Some reports say that .00001 percent or .00002 percent (or whatever) of the human race will survive. Varied regions of the earth won't shake too hard, they say. Other reports deny that. In any case, this event will be off the Richter scale. Don't even bother to hold on tight.

Predictably, people have resorted to a variety of coping mechanisms, some of which are depraved, others of which are enlightened. The word got out six weeks ago. The powers that be have been aware of this for years, but they kept things quiet to avoid mass hysteria. You could imagine their surprise when the town of Butler, Maine, blew itself up with a low-level nuclear reactor two days after the announcement. Talk about mass hysteria. "Maybe we shouldn't have given them six weeks," the powers probably shrugged.

They gave us the advanced warning with a charitable mindset, so we could quit our jobs, say our good-byes, start shooting heroin, plan a few orgies, that sort of thing. Again, the results have been split. Some have developed a glaring intimacy with the almighty. Others have drawn up "who to kill" check-lists and reached for their gun racks. We've even heard reports of a crazed lion tamer who's been touring small towns, introducing his pets to human meat. (I hate to be a Pollyanna, but I find that a little hard to swallow. Aren't tamers supposed to *tame*?) Several folks—who are clearly in the iron grip of denial—have gone about their routines, eating steak every Tuesday night, showing up at work even though the boss has shot himself, et cetera.

Suicide has become a trend. I never guessed that such a thing would be trendy, but the context has paved the way. The evening news ran a story on it. At the end of the story, the blonde anchorwoman climbed atop a ladder and hung herself. Talk about visual aids. On the whole, television has never been better. Our local weatherman appeared without pants the other morning. I don't recall him saying anything about weather. Needless to say, all programming schedules have gone out the window. Sometimes you tune in to shots of empty studios, sometimes sobbing pundits, mostly religious sermons. Given my knowledge that every second is precious, I'm trying not to watch too much TV. But sometimes it's hard to get off the couch. Sometimes there's very little blood flowing to my legs.

Most of my time is spent with my family: mother, father, younger sister, younger brother. We've been praying around the dinner table. Having lengthy philosophical discussions. Engaging in infinite hugs. We're all learning wild things about each other, not to mention ourselves. Mom dropped ecstasy the day after The Word got out. Dad admitted that he's been attracted to some males during his lifetime. I confessed that I found suicide tempting. They talked me out of it. They want to be looking in my eyes during the final moment, and me looking back at them. Because if there are no lights or tunnels or mystical beings, at least we'll have each other. At least we'll have the flesh-and-blood magnet that holds us together.

So I wait. I watch the meaningless clock. I have long talks with my friends. Try to read Buddhist books. Try to read Palahniuk. Smoke tons of marijuana. Eat tons of junk food. Masturbate constantly. Drive nowhere. Stay out of the frightening streets. And more than anything else: think about Selma. Despite the panic burning up my mind, somehow there's always room for Selma.

"I want to go to her," I tell my mother.

My mother knows how close we were. I see the understanding in her eyes.

My mother says, "You have to be here with us."

She says, "You should have thought of this before now."

I shrug and say, "I couldn't think clearly. Now I can see straight. I think Selma's the person I want to be with."

I can hear my mother's heart beating. She goes, "It's dangerous out there. You don't know how people will behave."

"It's a three-hour drive. Probably less since there's no traffic."

"How do you know there's no traffic?"

"Because everyone's at home. There's less than ten hours left."

We look at each other.

"You don't like it?"

"You know I don't like it."

But she follows that with, "But you have to make up your own mind. I'm not your protector anymore."

Suddenly I'm chilly. I don't need to hear that, but I know what she means. What use is a mother if she has no more days with which to raise you? She's no longer my mother. She's just the portal by which I entered this world. We've become peers. Everyone has.

Her eyes are moist.

"So, what're you gonna do now?" she asks me.

And so that's what I've been asking myself.

2.

I dial Selma's number. It's amazing how even on mankind's last day a phone call to a girl can still scare me. Or maybe I'm just scared to begin with.

Her sweet voice: "Hello?"

I grip my bedspread. Part of me wants to weep. She's still alive. No suicide conformity for her.

"Hello, Selma?"

It's been months. Feels like a year.

"Sean?"

Both of us breathing.

"I want to come to you, Selma."

I'm aware of the way this sounds: mannered, heavy, overly dramatic. But that's another recent trend. Everybody's over-the-top nowadays.

She laughs. Is it a real laugh or a nervous one? I ask myself that every time I hear someone laugh lately. Can anyone truly laugh?

"Shouldn't you be with your family?"

"Maybe. I don't know what the right thing to do is."

"Me neither."

"What are your plans?"

"To be here with my parents."

I think of my mother and father. They're downstairs in the kitchen, probably discussing my potential absence later on. "Would you not like it if I came?"

She laughs again. This time it's gotta be real.

"What's so funny?"

"It's all just so fast. How – are you?"

"Pretty terrible."

"Sounds familiar."

Every second we spend talking is worth more than gold. She knows this. Her pace is rapid. She says,

"Part of me thinks I'm hallucinating this conversation."

"Has that been happening to you? Have you been hallucinating?"

"I don't think so. But I've been trying to talk to spirits."

"Have you reached any?"

"Not sure. I see colors before I fall asleep."

In a flash, I picture red, yellow, green, blue, purple.

I say to her, "I haven't slept in days."

"Really?"

"No, I have. Just not for a long time. Couple hours here and there."

"You should try pills."

We share a pause. We both know that there'll be no more nights on which to try pills. She laughs a third time, very fake. She changes the topic: "Have *you* hallucinated?"

"No, but my little brother has. He thought he saw demons the other night."

"Maybe he did."

"You never know."

And you never will.

"My cousin in Texas is a little schizophrenic, too," Selma tells me. "She keeps asking her mom if this is all a conspiracy."

"It could be. That's what they think in the Middle East."

"Well, we'll find out tonight."

"Speaking of which, you have to tell me. We can't split hairs. We both have to be for it a hundred percent. Do you want me there?"

"Yes."

Tears slip down both sides of my face.

"I was prepared to say, 'Are you sure?' but I'm not going to."

"You know I'm sure."

"I love you, Selma."

She's crying now. Very hard. Funeral hard. "I love you, too. And I'm sorry, Sean. I'm so sorry."

She's either apologizing for breaking my heart or for the end of the world. Either way, she has my forgiveness.

"I know you are."

"When are you coming?"

"Now. Right now. It should only take me two or three hours."

"Be careful out there."

My mother's face flickers inside me.

"I will."

"Okay, I love you."

"I know. And Selma..."

"Yeah?"

"When I see you, I want to go inside you. I want to fuck you, if you think you're up to it."

More crying. "I think I am."

Her breath is hard. Somehow I can smell it. She smells like pure nature. Like the world before man. My whole body rings. I want to put my face in her neck. I want to feel her hips, her cheeks. The mere prospect of seeing her is worth getting killed for on the way.

My father is putting a gun in my hand. This is the gun that he told me didn't exist, the gun he never purchased, the one that *wasn't* hidden on the top shelf of his walk-in closet, in the white towel beside the shoebox. I've known he was lying since I was ten.

The piece is heavy on my palm. "Is it loaded?" I want to know.

"You think I'd give my child an unloaded gun?"

"Good point."

You have to hand it to my dad. Under the most extreme pressure imaginable, he still has the capacity for wit. I hug him. For his gun and his wit and everything else. I wish his body was warm, but it's not.

We look at each other. His face doesn't exist. He consists of two eyes. Their blue shade brings the Earth to mind. Kind of like a "before-and-after" setup. Right eye: Earth with people. Left eye: Earth without people. He blinks and the thought goes away.

We're touching each other's shoulders. It's nice to touch each other. Too bad we never connected like this before. Macho male bullshit. If we had known things would turn out this way, we would have been more physical. We've always been able to talk, but as I'm learning lately, touching transcends conversation.

"I can't say goodbye to you, Dad."

He smiles. "I'm gonna force you to. There's no way you'll leave without saying goodbye. I'll tie you up."

I pretend to laugh. "I could make it back in time for the end."

"No. You'll be in Selma's arms by then. You'll be too scared to move."

You'll be in Selma's arms. He's never spoken like that before. The birds and bees was never his thing. Whenever I brought girls home, he pretended they were all just my friends. Even when my door was locked and the radio was turned up loud.

He holds my hand. His palm is soaked. We haven't held hands in a long time. Between quick breaths, he says, "Let's go say goodbye to your mother."

3.

When I was in the first grade, some kids at school decided that I was ugly. To be honest, I've never felt that I was ugly. In fact, I tend to think the opposite. But those kids did a pretty good job of convincing me otherwise. The ringleader of the group went by the name of Peter. He was backed up by Jennifer, Allison, and some others whose names I don't recall. One day, while I was staring off into space, Peter turned around from the desk in front of me and asked me what I was looking at. I just shook my head. Then he said to "stop looking at me with your ugly face." Jennifer, Allison, and the no-names laughed. The u-word got repeated for the rest of the afternoon. I went home in an awful mood, but I said nothing to my parents, for I guessed that the torment was over.

The torment was only beginning. They went easy on me the next day—until lunchtime. Then, between bites of her cheese sandwich, with a gleeful smile, Jennifer said to Peter, "Hey, remember how Sean is 'ugly'?" Peter giggled and went to work on me again. I may have cried; I've blocked it out. In any case, I cried when I got home. My mother knocked on my bedroom door and asked me what was wrong. I told her the whole dreadful story. She demanded that I give her some names.

The next day, my mother picked me up from school. I usually rode the bus, but while my class was lined up at the curb, my mother appeared beside my teacher. She was like something out of a dream. It didn't make sense to me—school was the place where Mommy wasn't around—yet there she was. She asked my teacher, Mrs. Panensky, for a word in private, and the two of them stepped aside.

I never got called ugly again.

As a matter of fact, when I was a junior in high school, word got around that Jennifer intended to ask me to the prom. She chickened out, though, which was just as well, for I already had a date. Besides, Jennifer had long since devolved into a loser. I, on the other hand, was cool by then. Justice is sweet.

The fact that my mother intervened and told the teacher to reprimand those asshole kids didn't occur to me until a week after the looming apocalypse was announced. My brain's been turned inside out, so all kinds of repressed thoughts have been popping up. But even if this particular revelation had never occurred, I'd still perceive my mother as a hero.

Everything I've ever done, every choice I've ever made, every girl I've ever dated, every picture I've ever drawn, every course I've ever dropped, every fight I've ever picked—my mother has supported me. And now, in our sun-painted kitchen, she looks into my face and tells me that she doesn't mind that I'm gonna die with Selma.

"If that's your choice, Sean, I respect it."

Forget the meteorite. My mom's killing me already.

My tears won't stop. The insides of my cheeks are lined with mucous. We hug each other. Her body, unlike Dad's, is nice and warm. That's because women (in my humble opinion) are better at coping with stress. Something inside of men refuses to let go. Something inside of women understands when it's time to move on.

Her face is unreal. She's in her late forties, but she stopped aging at thirty-six. My friends always called her a M.I.L.F. ("Mother I'd Like to Fuck"). Some guys would be offended by that. I took it as a compliment. There are a lot worse things than being told your mother's hot.

I feel the bones in her upper back. She hasn't been eating lately. This is the last time I'll touch her, yet I don't want to overdo it. Because if you overdo it a little, you gotta overdo it a lot. Once you pass ten seconds, then you may as well keep hugging until thirty, then a minute, then the next thing you know everyone's been incinerated.

We move apart. Two wet faces. I resent her for a moment. The feeling cuts me up. She protected me from classroom bullies, but now she's letting the ultimate bully have its way with me. She should've turned on the oven before bed last night. She should've injected cyanide into my neck while I was sleeping. Anything but this.

Shut up. You know you want to go out like a champ.

"I'll be seeing you," she says.

Even though my father is behind me, I can see him grab his chest.

"Yeah," I stutter, "see you in another place."

I can't be sure that I believe this, but I know that she does, and that's all I need right now. She asks me, "Do you want to say goodbye to Josh and Erica?"

My brother and sister. They're in the basement playing video games. They know they won't be alive in a day, but their preadolescent minds are ignoring it.

My jaw is creaking. "No. No, I can't do that."

"Okay."

"It's just . . ."

"You don't have to explain."

"Tell them I love them."

"They know you do."

One more hug. This one's shorter, but its tightness makes it seem longer. I hope that I can take some of her warmth with me. I'll need it once I'm out there by myself.

As I exit the kitchen, my dad and I look at each other, both asking ourselves if another hug is called for. We mutually and telepathically decide against it. He asks me where the gun is. I tell him in my pants. He goes, "Don't use it unless you absolutely have to. Just because it's the last day doesn't mean you're allowed to go berserk."

I look to my mom for an inevitable second opinion. She nods. "He's right. But don't be naive, either. There could be lots of crazies out there."

"I'll be fine," I say.

Or at least as fine as I can be.

4.

"There could be lots of crazies out there."

Great. Just do this right. You have three quick stops to make before you get on the freeway, all of them local.

Before entering my hand-me-down '93 Ford Explorer (affectionately nicknamed "The Horse"), I check out the sky. Since word of the end got out, there's been talk about the weather. There's always talk about the weather, I guess. Even when we're all gone, the cockroaches will be bullshitting about the wind chill factor.

The sky is royal blue. Weeks back, some predicted rain. Others predicted wind. Some said fog. Snow. Hail. Sleet. Mist. Anything that evokes doom has been predicted. The truth is that this day is sublime. I don't even require a jacket.

I crank the engine on, toss my weapon into the passenger seat. Its scraped metal catches the sun. I turn on the radio. Static on most channels, but the classic rock station has blessed us all with round-the-clock psychedelics: Zeppelin, Hendrix, Morrison, The Grateful Dead, Franzschubert. I predict that every song I hear will be fueled by manic ambition. Anything to lift us from the darkness.

After I pull out of the driveway, I stop in the street and look at my house. The words "so long" drift from my lips. I depress the gas pedal and become one of the crazies out there.

5.

My first stop involves marijuana. I don't really have to stop for this, but I do so for sentimental reasons. I pull up behind my high school, in the parking lot next to the soccer fields. This is where my friends and I smoked every morning before homeroom during our senior year. I want the experience to be all pink with nostalgia, but it's dark black. There's no soothing me. My nerves are chewing each other up.

The marijuana should fix that—to an extremely limited extent. It doesn't make the pain go away; it just makes it difficult for me to string too many thoughts together. That makes moment-to-moment existence marginally more bearable. (The pressure of today will most likely crush the margin, but I'm trying to ignore that.) I sprinkle some opium on the weed. This, of course, enlarges the distance between me and reality. A couple years ago, right before winter break from college, I swore off chemicals of all kinds. I was determined to clean myself up en route to the real world. Silly me for assuming there would be one.

Instinct leads me to duck down below my car windows. Then it occurs to me that nobody who saw me would care. I haven't left the house in over two weeks, so I'm slightly behind on the latest etiquette.

I step outside and smoke up. Nobody's in sight. Force of habit leads me to feel vulnerable, but that feeling passes once the chemicals hit my brain. "I am smoking weed and opium right now," I say out loud, too loud, pronouncing every word with arrogant meticulousness. "I am smoking weed and opium, and I now intend to piss on the wall of my school."

There's liquor in my belly from last night. I've been using it to fall asleep. I spray dark urine on the school's red brick wall. My pants and boxers are around my knees. Fuck any onlookers. If they've never seen anything this strange, then they will in just eight short hours anyway.

I want the act of pissing to free me. I want to feel spirited and rebellious and juiced-up and strong, but I feel like a weak little flea. Just as I start to envision fleas, the opiates redirect my thoughts: Go see Uncle Joey.

Uncle Joey isn't *my* uncle. He's merely the owner of Uncle Joey's Diner, one of the hotspots in my little town. The man is a harrowing denial case. He's carrying on like nothing's changed. He opens shop at six a.m., throws some eggs on the stove, twirls around the OPEN/CLOSED sign, and goes to work. (Fortunately for everyone, he stopped accepting money around ten days ago. That's the only indication that he knows what's up.) I've eaten there a few times in the past six weeks. Uncle Joey does a reasonably good job of approximating the atmosphere of an actual, non-doomed restaurant. One day, this illusion was cracked when one of the patrons started raping his wife in a corner booth, but Joey chased them off with his shotgun. Minor disturbance.

I like Uncle Joey. Despite the recent absence (or fading, I guess) of pupils in his eye sockets, I'm not afraid of him. And just in case I do become afraid of him, I've got Dad's pistol on me. I stuff the piece in my pants before leaving my car. Its cold steel offends my relatively warm dick.

"Hi, Uncle Joey," I fake-smile as I pull up a stool.

"Well, hello there, Sean! I haven't seen you in a while!"

The old man is screaming at me, but I'm used to it. It's his way of showing affection. I yell back, "Yeah! I haven't seen you either!" but he doesn't get my joke.

"What can I get for you today?"

"Just something to get my sugar up. Maybe a blueberry muffin."

"Mmmm, sounds good. Coming right up!"

I turn around. There are not many others in attendance. Scattered couples and loners. It occurs to me that I could shoot everyone here and no one could ever touch me for it. I wonder how the bureaucrats in Heaven would handle that case: "Gee, this is a tough one we've got here. He was a saint throughout most of his life, but he went fucking ballistic on the last day. Should we send him back to Earth for another try? Oh, wait! There is no more Earth!"

A muffin is in front of me. It looks like a bruised, bleeding fist. I lift it from its plate and rise from the stool. "Not gonna stay here today?" Uncle Joey asks me.

"Nah, I'm in a hurry. Thanks."

"You sure you don't want a glass of milk?"

That sounds good. I tell him so.

I return to my seat. The weed-and-seeds combo is doing a nice job. Everything is liquid. Namely the milk that Joey places in front of me. I pick up the cold glass and start moving toward the door.

"Hey!"

My heart snaps. I spin around. Joey has daggers where his eyes belong. He says, "You're not gonna steal my glass, are you?"

Suddenly I'm screaming. Everyone's looking at me. They're not shocked or offended or anything; they're just looking. I go, "You're not gonna ever need this fucking glass, you fucking idiot!"

Uncle Joey is reaching down behind the bar. That's where he keeps his shotgun. I throw the glass of milk right at him. Maybe it hits his face, maybe his chest. I hear it break on some part of him as I run out the front door.

6.

Given my little outburst, it's a good thing I planned on stopping by the Meditation Circle. Something resembling guilt is circling my brain. (It's closer to regret than out-and-out guilt.) I shouldn't have thrown the glass, but then again the fucker could have shot me. Whatever; I'm an asshole. I hope I didn't hurt him. Today is a day for virtue, not sin. Hence my decision to visit the Circle.

The Circle is over at the local library. They pushed all the bookshelves to the walls to create a wide-open space. In that space, at any given time, three hundred or so of my fellow townspeople can be found holding hands. They engage in group meditation for a while, then stop and trade thoughts and fears, then engage again. I've avoided the scene until now. My mother tried to encourage me to go, but I told her my hands were too sweaty to partake.

Right now, my hands have crumbs and blueberry on them, but I'm sure nobody will mind. I wipe them on my pant legs, stash the gun in the glove, and head inside.

Fact: Even in the final hours, libraries remain quiet.

Everybody's eyes are closed. Some faces are divided by tear streaks. The fluorescent lights make the tears glow. A few heads are thrown back, but most hang down. I don't know what the protocol for inclusion is, but there's no time for politeness. I step between two little boys. My brother and sister come to mind. The opiates sweep them away.

The next thing I know, I'm in my least favorite place: my head. It's louder than a construction site in here. My eyes are closed tight, and my eyeballs are making an asserted effort to break through their lids. I picture open mouths and sharp teeth. Don't panic, I tell myself. Then my chest starts to tighten. What am I doing here? I belong among the people I love. Stop it. You love *all* people. No you don't! You're so full of—

A female voice interrupts my introverted nightmare. "Does anybody want to share what you experienced?"

The whole room stirs.

You could imagine my surprise when the little kid to my right starts talking. Cute kid: glasses, striped shirt, messy hair. Probably knows what being picked on is all about. In a chirping, tiny voice, he goes, "I saw lots of bright lights."

The lady speaks again, and this time I'm able to locate her. She's an aging hippie, in her early forties. A modest potbelly sticks out against her faded purple top. Her smile brings her whole face to life. She says to the kid, "That's good. Any neat colors?"

I picture red, yellow, green, blue, purple.

The kid says, "Like mostly gold."

I realize that nobody is still holding hands except for me and the kid. Instinct tells me to let go, but when I try to he holds on tighter. Suddenly I feel very protective of him.

"Gold. Mmmm, that's a nice one. Where do you think it came from?"

"I think from this man standing next to me."

Have you ever had six hundred eyes staring at you? I don't recommend it. A thunderstorm erupts in my chest. Even though I regret yelling at the diner, I feel like doing so again. After all, it felt good at the time. I should say to them, "You fucking maniacs! How can you all stand here like this? How can anybody do anything?"

But of course I would never do that. Some of these people know my mother.

I smile and shrug. The hippie lady looks at me. "Have you joined us here before?"

"No. First time. My mother—"

A voice that I can't locate chimes in: "His mother is Rena from the hair salon."

"Oh," says the hippie, "I *thought* you looked familiar."

Never too late for some small talk, huh?

"I just wanted to stop by and see what this is all about."

"It's all about whatever you want it to be about."

"Oh, that's pretty cool."

I know she's gonna say it before she does: "What do you want it to be about?"

Human nature is some vicious beast. Despite the extremity of the circumstances, social conditioning leads me to be shy. I reach inside and try to break through. The awkward silence is of epic proportions. The little kid pumps my hand. I look at his face. He seems to feel protective of me, too.

I look back to the hippie. "I want to experience something grand."

Some mutters and nods. These people actually understand me. And even if they don't understand me, they're at least validating me. My chest unwinds.

"Go on," the hippie says.

"Well, there's a lot of grandness in the world. Buildings and statues and skyscrapers"—it occurs to me that skyscrapers *are* buildings, but I'm doing okay otherwise—"and political ideas and religions and great works of art, and all these things are wonderful, but I can't feel them. I mean, I can *feel* them, but they don't reach all the way in. And I want to experience something that reaches all the way in."

Many of the elders seem impressed. I've always wanted to give a lecture.

"And this thing that's about to happen, it certainly reaches all the way in. It rattles all of us very deep. But it's not grand. It's not grand because it's dark. It's twisted and ugly. And grand things are full of light. They're exciting, not depressing."

The hippie is falling in love with me. "Would you mind telling us what kind of a 'grand thing' you're looking for?"

I saw that one coming also. Something inside me wants to plead the fifth, but something stronger persists: "Well, I'm only twenty-three, and I never got a chance to feel like a person."

The kid holding my hand doesn't know what I mean, but he's listening.

"I never got a chance to have an identity. I mean, I think I have virtues. I think I'm a bright kid, and I like to draw and paint, and I think I'm pretty nice and I make people feel good about themselves, but I never got a chance to do anything. I never had my turn."

This isn't sufficient. The hippie's eyes are thirsty. She wants to know "like what?"

So I say, "And I think if I had had my turn, I could've been pretty good. I could've been a leader or a known artist or something. And maybe that would have been grand. To give the grand thing instead of just receiving it. *That* would reach all the way in. Not because it would make my ego feel good. Well, it would, but . . ."

That gets an unexpected laugh.

". . . more importantly, it would be good for other people. Their lives would possibly be enriched, even if only for a second. And that would be powerful. Not just for me, but for the ones I'm touching."

I'm worried that I sound like an egomaniac, so I throw on some humility: "The thing is, people have touched me a lot, and I used to take that for granted. And I hate myself for taking it for granted and never giving anything back. Because if I'd just been able to give something back, I think it could have been special. But no, I had to waste my time doing drugs and hanging out with my friends and thinking about girls. Once in a while, I gave a dollar to a homeless person, or sent my grandmother a card, but that was it. And I'm pissed. I'm fucking *pissed*, and I guess I feel guilty and helpless."

My use of the f-word seems to surprise only me. People are busy registering what I've said. I never thought I'd say *fuck* loudly in a library, and I can't say that I'm touched by the honor.

The hippie goes, "Perhaps you've done something grand just now?"

I smile at her. Sweet lady. It's good of her to try to placate me. But I can't accept that. "That wasn't grand. I've got so much more in me. And pretty soon there won't *be* a me. And what am I supposed to do then?"

"You're still here now . . ."

Many smiles and nods.

"You can still do something."

I wonder if the little boy feels me shake.

The hippie lady stares at me, into me, through me, and asks, "What are you going to do with the rest of your time?"

I tell the hippie lady, and the boy who's got my hand, and all the others, and all the world, "I'm gonna go see this girl I know. I've been angry with her for a while, but I'm gonna go see her anyway. And I'm gonna love her. I'm gonna love her so much that all her pain and fear will go away."

7.

As it turns out, my confession is among the least melodramatic. I stick around and listen to some others. There's an aging cancer survivor who laments about the irony of dying so soon after she was cured; a mustached tough guy who says he really wants to kill his sister-in-law before the day's out, but he's forcing himself not to do so; a traumatized twenty-something (who I actually knew back in high school when she wore a miniskirt and threw around pompoms) who says she "feels responsible" for the end of the world. I leave right after that one. No time for glaring ridiculousness.

On my way out the door, I feel a hand tug at my back pocket. I turn around to see my little friend with the glasses and the stripes. He asks me if I'm gonna kiss the girl that I'm visiting. I laugh out loud. This laugh is real.

"Why? Do you think I should?"

The kid nods quickly. "Is she pretty?" he wants to know.

I put a hand on his shoulder and lean in close to him: "This girl's prettier than anybody you've ever seen."

The kid's mouth drops open. He says, "Then you should *definitely* kiss her."

"The question is not whether I'll kiss her. The question is whether I'll be able to *stop* kissing her."

"That's true," the kid says, as if he knew I would come up with that.

"Wish me luck?"

"Good luck."

We hug each other. See you next lifetime.

8.

I met Selma in my dorm hallway. She was wearing her pajamas. I was waiting behind her to use the water fountain. It was the middle of the night. When she was done drinking water, she turned and faced me. Her face was peaked yet amazing. We'd never seen each other before, yet she spoke to me like we went way back:

"Can you feel my forehead and see if I'm hot?"

My response didn't require much introspection. "Yeah, sure."

Twelve words between us, and already I was touching her.

She *was* hot. Temperature-wise and otherwise. I resisted sharing this pun with her. I just told her she was hot. I gave the h-word a little emphasis to flatter her subconscious. The next thing I knew, we were walking to the campus convenience store. I treated her to orange juice. She thanked me with a high-five, told me she was a Political Science major. I told her I was an Art major. She didn't mock that like most people do. No little jokes about how I'd end up poor. In fact, she dug my work. In greater fact, she made my work better.

We became attached. Worshipped one another. Talked nonstop. Argued. Debated. Begged. Pleaded. Swung on the swing-set at the park. Ate off each other's forks. Check-listed every cliché.

She was the second female I'd ever met who told me I was good-looking on a daily basis (the first one gave birth to me). She had a thing for touching my cheeks. Not squeezing them like a psychotic relative, just touching them with quiet curiosity. This got annoying when I hadn't shaved. Otherwise, I let her leave her prints all over me.

Her body was a masterpiece. She liked to be on top. I swooned over the slight protrusion of her ribcage, the paleness of her skin. Not pale like paper, more like white rose petals. Her nipples were nearly flesh-tone. I'd never seen that before. One of them always got slightly harder than the other. I equated this to the fact that she was left-handed (don't ask me why). She wore button-down shirts. I liked asking her to unbutton them in front of me. She always obliged. Even if we were in the hall.

But it wasn't the eroticism that got me; it was the closeness. Before her, I thought I knew all about closeness. Before me, so did she. But we broke through to something new together. We somehow managed to travel very deep inside each other— beyond so many walls and fences, so much chain-link and barbed wire—without judging one another. We liked each other too much for judgment. And eventually, we loved each other.

It was snowing outside. Class was cancelled for days. It felt like weeks. (Every day at college felt like three.) We hung out in her dorm room. Her roommate had gone home early for winter break. It was the greatest sleepover in history. We outdid every clique of twelve-year-old girls that ever stayed up all night making marshmallows and doing each other's hair.

We smoked too much pot on the first night. Blew the stuff in each other's mouths and nostrils. I expressed concern that we were leaning on the pot too much. It was keeping us from authentically bonding. She agreed without hesitation. We donated my stash to the fake punk rockers down the hall. You should've seen the look on their faces. It was like paradise had pulled up to their doorstep. Selma and I went over there together, like Ozzie and Harriet delivering a crumb cake to the new neighbors. She held the pot; I held the rolling papers. They thanked us for three straight semesters.

Then we went home (meaning back to her room) and pressed our faces against each other's stomachs. Spent hours on the carpet. Watched one DVD after another: Scorsese, Spielberg, Hitchcock, Peter Weir, the Coen Brothers. Analyzed the characters. Laughed at all the same parts. Agreed that DeNiro was selling out. Made up our own ghost stories. Hers were always more funny than they were scary. Silly stuff about rabbits carrying axes. She made me soup on her portable stove. Fed the first spoonful to me, then I had to take over before she spilled it. She got mad that I didn't trust her. Then I told her I loved her. No build-up, no fanfare. The most natural thing in the world. She said it back to me. Our eyes became glazed; sub-visible tears. I kissed her over and over. Got to know her mouth. How her bottom teeth were a little crooked even though she'd once worn braces. If her teeth were straight, she wouldn't be nearly as perfect.

Everybody knew us. Holding hands en route to class. Occupying booths in the dining hall. Standing on opposite sides of crowded elevators. Eyeing each other. Communicating without talking. She called me old-fashioned when I winked at her. I called her newfangled when she opened doors for me.

And then, two years into our relationship and one month before graduation, Selma got drunk one night and fucked this kid named Brian.

But I don't want to think about that now.

9.

My parents gave me the Ford Explorer just before I went away to college. Best gift I've ever received. All my friends asked if I was gonna name it. I always glared at them and told them that was stupid. But then—wouldn't you know it?—an attachment developed. I began admiring this piece of machinery. The car has a subtle nobility to it. A distinct no-kidding-around vibe comes from its levers and switches. It's warm, clean, and roomy, and its hood juts forward like the symmetrical nose of a handsome face.

The nickname came out of nowhere (which is where all the truest nicknames come from). Whenever I was looking for my Explorer in a parking lot, for some reason I'd think of Richard III crying, "A horse! My kingdom for a horse!" I'd mutter that to myself as I searched for the car. And then, once The Horse came into view, I'd change it up a bit: "My horse! A kingdom for my horse!"

I pet the dash and whisper, "That's right, baby. That's right."

My horse deserves a kingdom. Especially since it will outlive me.

10.

I'm convinced that the whole "time flies when you're having fun" theory is a crock of shit. Time can also fly when you're miserable. It's almost noon yet I'm just hitting the interstate. Roughly seven hours till the fall. Good thing my instincts were correct: The freeway is empty. It belongs to me and The Horse. We're the only idiots with these kinds of plans. I put my seatbelt on and kick the beast up to 100.

The weed/opium cocktail is thinning out. I feel insane. Clinically speaking, I probably am insane. Me and everybody else who's not hiding under a rock. The fact that I can think is astounding. Our brains are really something else. No matter how aware you are of the big picture, part of you will remain entangled in the smaller details: hands on steering wheel; bugs on windshield; tension in forehead; gun in glove compartment; bleeding female on the pavement.

"Fuck!"

The Horse nearly spins when I hit the brakes.

It's awfully sticky out here. I look north, then south. Winding, barren concrete. I've never stood in the center lane of a freeway before. The female is less than six feet away from my front tires. Her hair is naturally blonde but presently red. (Or at least the side that hit the pavement is red; I can't see the other side.) She's wearing overalls, a white long-sleeved T-shirt, and no shoes. I approach her with caution.

(Turn around. Go home. Hug your mother. Say goodbye to Selma on the phone.)

Dry coughs pound from her throat. In a snap, she looks up at me. Her eyes are light blue. I feel like running, but I freeze instead. Her face is bloody but not cut. The wound is somewhere on her scalp; that's where the red is darkest.

Maybe I'm hallucinating. A lot of people have experienced sensory distortion lately. She seems very real and tactile, but the drugs I smoked are creating waves everywhere, and nothing can be fully trusted. In any case, hallucination or not, she/it is speaking to me:

"Please help me."

I think I hear a car behind me. I turn around: nothing but The Horse. It seems to be grinning. Good boy. Stick with me. Back to the female.

"What happened?"

I'm not stepping any closer. I can't see her hands; she could have a knife—or worse. The eyes in the back of my head glance through my windshield. Fucking idiot; I should go get my gun. I turn around again. Then she speaks to my back, and her voice is coming from somewhere new. She's standing.

I say, "Hold on a second," as I whip back toward her. I circle around to my passenger side door, grip the handle.

"Do you have water?" she asks.

"No. No water here." But that would have been a good idea.

My hands are in my glove box. Ah, there's my little pal. Thanks for holding onto her, Horsie. I stick the thing in the top of my ass crack.

She's coming toward me. I note that she's attractive, despite all the blood. Her palms are facing me: empty. I scan her pockets: no bulges or shines. My heart slows down a little. Take control of the situation.

"What happened to you?"

She comes over to me and hugs me. This is now Hug-A-Stranger Day. The blood from her head stains my gray shirt. I don't exactly mind. To be honest, the physical contact calms me down even more. She loosens the hug and looks into me. "It was so bad."

"Here, come with me."

I take her hand, turn us around, and guide her into the passenger seat. From zero to trusting in three seconds, huh, Sean? Fuck it. If she were dangerous, she wouldn't have been bleeding in the street.

Leaving her door open, I circle around The Horse and return to my saddle. Suddenly she's spilling her story: "There's a bus with women on it. We have to go catch them."

"A bus with women?"

She's crying. Hard. Her guts are involved. "These two fucking assholes drove around grabbing women and taking them onto this bus. They've been driving us around for two days and throwing us off. My turn just happened."

I'm getting feverish. "How long ago was this?"

"Like five minutes."

And then God must have said, "Send in Sean."

"You have to go after them."

"What do you mean, 'go after them'?"

Her scream drowns out the radio: "There's two other women on that fucking bus! Get moving!"

I do no such thing. "What are we gonna do?"

"I don't know! Fucking shoot them or something!"

"How are we gonna do that?"

The blonde's hand is shining. That's because she has my pistol. Imaginary bullets punch through my skull. "Give me that."

"Huh?"

"Give me my gun back, and I'll take you wherever—"

The gun is on my slippery palm. Catastrophe averted. My heart belches. "Why did you take that from me?"

She shrugs. "I didn't know if you were safe."

"And now you do know?"

"I could tell by the way you sat me down."

We smile at each other. There's blood on her teeth. Our collective breath fogs up my windshield. "We should get you to a hospital."

More volume: "No! Fucking step on it! You're not letting those girls die!"

Either my head is spinning or the world is revolving faster. (If the latter is true, maybe the meteorite will miss.)

The Horse mutters to me, "Let's go, Sean."

Now I'm hallucinating.

Through the air vents, The Horse says, "I would like to go do this."

I need more weed. Or less. I click the gear to *D* and floor the fucker.

"What do you wanna do?" I ask. "Blow their tires out?"

I think I'm being sarcastic, but she seems to take it as an earnest suggestion. "Maybe," she exhales. "Just get to it. They won't leave the freeway."

I'm having an out-of-body experience. The Horse and the blonde have seized control. "So who are these fucks?" I ask her.

"I have no idea. They hate women. They held knives to our necks."

I check out her neck. No apparent cuts, just lots of blood.

"Can I offer you some pot?" I ask, being hospitable. It's the opposite of water, but it might ease her pain.

"No, I'm fine. Thanks."

I nod. Great. She's fine, I'm fine, everybody's fine.

My gas pedal touches the carpeting. We blast up the road. Trees become blurs at our sides. I free one hand and find my bowl between the seats. I hand her the lighter and ask her to blaze me up. Given the looks of her scalp, I hope she gets a secondhand buzz.

"Can you drive like that?" she wants to know.

"I drive *better* like this," I brag.

The Horse corrects me: "I'm the one doing all the driving."

11.

"There it is!"

Apparently she got no buzz. She's still yelling. Her pink fingernail taps the windshield as she points. There's a plump white dot up ahead. I feel like crying for my mother. The opiates have barely dented my anxiety. Ladies and Gentleman . . . welcome to "Opium vs. Crisis Situation." Who—will—win?

"Do these guys have guns?" I ask her, studying the weapon in my lap. It looks like a horizontal robot penis.

"No, they're small-time. Just a couple pricks."

I'm not sure if she digs vulgarity, but I try her out: "The only weapons they use are their pricks?"

She glares at me. Fantastic eyes. But her mouth is frowning. "They didn't rape us," she says.

Ouch. "No, that's not what I— "

"I don't even think they like sex."

"I didn't mean . . . I was just playing on words." (Too much opium.)

"Well, kid, if you'll forgive me for saying so, I'm not in the mood to play."

"Right. Sorry."

I imagine that most people whose heads are bleeding aren't in the mood to play. I keep that thought to myself. "What's your name?" I ask her. A more mainstream attempt at breaking the ice.

"Paula. How 'bout you?"

"Sean."

"Nice to meet you."

"Nice meeting you."

The white dot grows and grows.

"You from around here?"

It's never too late for small talk.

"No. I'm from Florida. Those fucks dragged me across the country."

Paula doesn't ask me where I'm from. Under normal circumstances, this would piss me off, but I imagine she's lingering on the thought of being kidnapped.

"What are we gonna do when we see these guys?"

Paula squints through my buggy windshield, shoots imaginary lasers at the bus. "One of us is gonna have to shoot 'em."

My ability to swallow disappears. Rocks squeeze against the inside of my forehead. "Which one of us?" I ask, seeking maternal guidance.

"I guess I'll do it. It's my deal."

She's fucking-A right about that.

"You just have to pull up next to them."

My lungs are trafficking less air than usual. "Um, Paula . . ."

"What?"

"Maybe you should think about this."

"I've taken care of that already."

She's a fucking gunslinger with the lines, this lady.

"You're talking about killing people."

"I wouldn't define these people as people."

"What would you define them as?"

"Like ants."

My right hand leaves the steering wheel and conducts my speech: "I don't want to sound like a preacher here, but what would *God* define them as?"

The white dot has officially become a bus.

"You believe in that shit?"

"I don't know."

"So, what do you care about God?"

"Because He may be out there."

Paula grinds her teeth.

I add, "Or She."

"Or whatever," she snaps, apparently unconcerned with any sexism on my part. "If there was a God, why would He be ending the fucking world?"

"Because maybe He's got other plans. Maybe the human thing has worn out its welcome."

"Well, okay. Be that as it may, we're all gonna go anyway. We may as well deny these scumbags the freedom to go out with everyone else."

She's making sense. No, fuck that. I wince and shake my head. It's military rhetoric she's using. Too many militants down there in Florida. Pitching justice and all that shit. *An eye for an eye.* I can't be taken in by that. Not at this late date. "But Paula, since we're all gonna go, what's the use of settling scores on the way out?"

"But *Sean*, if we're all gonna go, what's the use of not going out like a champion?"

I nearly veer into the woods. That's *my* expression. The air vents smile at me.

One never knows what form one's tests will take. Is this my glorious shot? A bleeding justice freak and a misogyny bus?

"Besides," Paula says, "we need to disable them *somehow*."

"How come?"

"Because you're out of gas and we're gonna need a car."

An avalanche crumbles through my head. I check out the gauges. The needle's well below *E*.

"Shit," I say. "I forgot to feed The Horse!"

Paula looks at me like I have ten heads. I wish I did. Anything to get out of this one.

12.

The white bus is no longer an abstract concept. It's a massive, rolling, belching, filthy monster, less than a hundred yards away. The license plate says Louisiana. These guys have taken their little sport quite a distance. At the rate they're going, they could make it up to New England before the end. But not if Paula has anything to say about it.

"Here's what we do," she tells me.

This "we" shit is getting to me. I'm content to remain her chauffeur.

"You gotta pull up alongside them and pretend you're as nasty and fucked up as they are. These guys aren't incredibly sharp; they'll definitely buy it."

"How am I supposed to pretend that?"

"I don't know, Sean. Be creative. Pull my hair and pinch me. I'll make like I'm all crying and hurt."

"That second part shouldn't be hard."

"No shit. Can you do that?"

I nod a little, reluctant to seal the pact verbally. "Then what?"

"You roll down the window and yell, 'I say we toss this bitch again, fellas!'"

"You're telling me they're gonna fall for this? They're gonna assume that you told me what they did?"

"Yeah, or *you* can tell them I told you. Or maybe you witnessed it. Whatever."

"This is totally transparent. It's like Superman wearing glasses and everyone believing he's Clark Kent."

Paula stares me down. To her, my pop cultural reference is more childish than the notion of murdering people. "Look," she says, "if they don't fall for it, at least we tried."

My shoulders are so tense that they're almost touching my earlobes. I say, "So the concept is, they're gonna pull over for the sake of recruiting me as part of their team and throwing you again."

"Right. And as they come near us, we blow their brains out."

My foot nearly slips off the gas pedal. "Okay, that's the part that gives me pause."

Paula shakes with frustration. "Fine, kid, I'll take care of it then."

"This *is* your vendetta. I'm just driving."

"Yeah, you're what's called an accomplice."

She seasons some extra salt onto the a-word. It's enough to stop my heart. I look at her. Those pinkish teeth are in view; she's grinning. Paula must have been head of her sorority. I'm sure her spirits soared when hazing season rolled around.

We're nearly parallel to the bus.

"I just have different values than you, is all," I mumble.

"Same here," she breathes.

I have no tolerance for violence. She has no patience for pussies.

"Start acting like an asshole," she tells me.

I already feel like one.

13.

"You terrible fucking cunt!"

I've got a soggy handful of Paula's red hair. She's an excellent actress; if I'm not mistaken, actual tears are dripping down her face. Her back is facing the passenger side window. She kicks her bare dirty feet at me. The gun is under my ass, jabbing it full of holes.

"Fuck you, scumbag!" she cries. "Let me go! I hate you!"

"Shut up! Shut the fuck up!"

This is reasonably cathartic. I feel closer to DeNiro.

The speedometer reads 110. The Horse doesn't go any faster. There's a strong possibility that we'll stall for the lack of gas, but I should have enough in the reserve tank for five more minutes. Hopefully the ants will catch on by then.

I see two silhouettes through the driver's side window, and two more in the back. The front two have short hair and the back two have long hair. Paula spoke the truth. I wait for the head that's driving to turn our way. Come on, dipshit, you probably haven't seen another car for hours, if not days.

I shift gears in our fake fight: "What if they don't look our way?!" I scream, shaking a tight fist toward Paula.

Paula blinks before she catches on. Kicking at me, she yells, "They *will*!"

"I don't know about that!"

My face is mean, ugly.

"Be an optimist!" she commands me.

"There's no such thing anymore!"

"Yeah?! I thought you believed in Heaven!"

"The vote's still out on that!" I shriek, ramming The Horse's dashboard.

Voila. The driver looks at us. His jaw moves. He's talking to his friend/partner/brother. Said f/p/b rises from his passenger seat. More chatter. Hurry the hell up, guys.

"They're looking!" I scream.

"Good! Keep it up! You deserve a fucking Oscar!"

"You too, you goddamn slave!"

"Fuck you, you thankless fucking captor!"

The two male silhouettes are taking us in. I can't see their eyes, but I'm sure they're open wide. When you toss someone from a moving car, you don't expect her to turn up again, let alone this way.

I move into phase two: rolling down Paula's window. My hand rattles as I click the button to the left of the steering wheel. The wind slices Paula's bloody hair. "Are they rolling their window down?!" she screams.

"Keep your fucking mouth shut! They might!"

Paula's eyes are thoughtful as she takes this in. It occurs to both of us that my words were half in and half out of character.

A yellow warning light appears beside my fuel gauge.

The driver-silhouette's shoulder is rotating. A line of darkness appears at the top of his window. I whisper, "He's rolling it down."

These guys look pretty gentle for a pair of scumbags. They both sport pale baby faces. Despite their status as lowlifes, they have not a beard or mustache between them. And from my vantage point, it looks like they should lay off the cheeseburgers. (Within the next six and a half hours, of course.) Their baby mouths hang open in shock. If I'm not mistaken, they look slightly offended. Maybe I've deviated from their rulebook. I hope there's not a point penalty.

I lock eyes with the driver, then swallow for the first time since I found Paula. Paula ups the screaming and struggling. My eardrums retract. I yell out, "Hey! I think you gentleman left some trash out on the freeway!"

The fatsoes start whistling and heehawing. How it must pleasure psychos to find others just like them. I wonder how these two hooked up. The driver calls out, "Yep, looks like she's been recycled!"

The passenger howls with laughter. They engage in some kind of secret hand-slap.

Paula interjects, "You guys are all going to fucking hell for this!"

The driver corrects her: "This *is* hell, baby. This *is* hell!"

I let loose the first and final "Heehaw!" of my life. Then I go, "Hey, our little girlfriend here told me what you guys cooked up. You mind letting me have a toss? I don't have enough height over here!"

The psychos lock eyes. Paula and I freeze—she with mock horror, me with mock curiosity. The warning light blinks.

Then, for the second time in my life, I hear a human being invite me to come harm another human being: "Sure, pal! Pull over to the shoulder!"

Paula's black hatred seems suddenly reasonable.

"You like beer?" the passenger calls to me. His voice is squeaky.

I say, "Hell yeah, man! But I'm pretty fucked up to begin with!"

14.

The shoulder. We sit thirty feet behind the bus.

My Adam's apple is the size of a peach. I'm not sure if I'll be able to stand and walk. I think my adrenal glands are tapped out.

Paula goes, "Give me the gun."

I obey. My ass sighs with relief.

She's all business, this Paula: "I'm gonna hold the gun behind my back. You make like you're holding my hands together. Then when we get close to them, I'll let loose in their ugly faces."

"I can't do this."

"Shut up."

"I'm sorry they hurt you."

"They went *beyond* hurting me."

"I'm weak. I've never done anything. I'll screw up."

The bus's front right-hand door swings open. Out comes the driver. I was wrong about the cheeseburger thing. The guy looks like he eats ponies.

I put on my angry, villainous face. As if I'm reprimanding her, I say, "Only one of them is coming. The other's probably watching the women."

"Fuck him. He can't hide in there."

"But he can kill your friends."

"They're not my friends," Paula says, efficiently departing from the point.

The driver is very close to us. I can see his chest hair above the collar of his tank top. His expression is equal parts vicious and bemused.

At the top of my lungs, I scream, "Let's go, you bitch!"

Paula's holding the gun with both hands behind her back. I grab onto it like it's a handle, open my door, and drag her outside. We're both careful to keep Paula's front facing the driver. The air out here is too hot for words.

He's ten feet away. Eight feet. Six.

"She's some feisty bitch, this one!" I note.

"Tell me about—"

The driver has a third eye. It's red and smoking. Birds fly from trees. My hands are empty. Paula is running toward the bus door. Two females and one male scream. The driver falls backwards. His blood crawls beneath my feet.

Something in me wants to hide, but my nervous system is not game for motion. I let the man's blood stain the soles of my shoes. My neck creaks as I tilt my head up. Paula's aboard the bus. The dusty windows make the scene black-and-white. She's aiming the gun. I tense up for another shot. The clouds pause in the sky.

Nothing happens. Nothing but screams:

"I'll cut this fucking bitch's throat!"

"Let her go!"

"I'll do it right now!"

"You don't have the balls!"

My equilibrium is fucked. Despite the blood on the ground, I could lie down right here. Then my Horse addresses me from behind: "Help her, Sean."

"I can't."

"*Help her.*"

"I'm too young."

"That doesn't mean anything."

My eyes take a break during the few seconds in which I board the bus. I see nothing but my own churning thoughts. Then I'm onboard. Inventory: Paula standing at the foot of the aisle, aiming gun; dark-skinned woman ducking and crying in backseat; bland-looking fat man standing mid-aisle, facing Paula; Caucasian female, short brown hair, in bland man's arms; carving knife at Caucasian woman's throat; every mouth open, noisy.

The bland man's eyes are on me. "You're a pretty good actor, aren't you?"

Paula doesn't know I'm behind her. She and I both say, "No shit."

Paula turns toward me briefly, too briefly to communicate anything. The bland man takes a step forward, bringing the Caucasian with him. When Paula spins back toward him, he freezes again.

Then I realize something that Paula doesn't. I don't want to be a killer, or even an accomplice, but I'd be dumb to keep this thought to myself.

"Um, Paula . . ." I say.

"What?"

"There was only one bullet in that gun."

The bus goes quiet. I feel Paula's body temperature drop. The bland man lets go of the Caucasian and charges Paula.

"Shoot him now!" I yell.

Paula drives a bullet through the bland man's neck. Red dots streak the walls and windows, and the man slams onto the floor.

I say to his body, "I'm a pretty *great* actor, actually."

15.

The tip of my dad's gun is smoking. I have to tell Paula to lower her aim as she faces me. She obliges and apologizes. "That was some chance you took," she exhales.

The two other women breathe and shake.

"Not really," I shrug, hiding my panic beneath a thin veneer of nonchalance. "His only reason for holding the knife was to keep you from shooting him. Once I made him think you weren't a threat, he was bound to let go of her." I point to the brown-haired Caucasian.

"What if I hadn't caught on when you said 'shoot'?" Paula wants to know.

"I knew you were quick enough."

Paula digs my compliment. "You're a good judge of character."

"Yeah, that and fifty cents will get me a cup of coffee."

Paula goes, "Coffee is free nowadays."

16.

I spend three precious minutes of my life telling Paula not to leave her captors' bodies in the middle of the freeway. "Another car could come," I tell her. "You don't fuck with the dead," I tell her.

I say to her, "Their bodies weren't guilty, only their souls."

Paula nods at that last one, even though she claimed not to believe in God. Maybe she believes in souls but not God. No time to worry about that. The four of us roll the two bodies into the woods. The bland one lands on top of the fat one. Two peas in a pod. Whether the apocalypse killed them or we killed them, they were bound to spend eternity together.

The famous question returns: What now? It's hard to prioritize. Do we find some water to drink? Clean off Paula's wound? Clean off Paula's wound with the water we find? As I interrogate myself by the side of the freeway, the Caucasian holds her hand out. "Lisa," she says.

"Sean," I reply.

I can't tell whose hands are wetter when we shake.

"Thank you for that," she says.

"It was nothing," I tell her. And I truly believe that. Our little showdown was of no consequence.

Paula continues to believe otherwise. The act of killing didn't rewire her moral compass. She stands near the trees and squints into the woods, toward the red and beige pile of flesh and bone, and mumbles, "Bastards." I can see where she's coming from, but I still can't catch my breath.

"I gotta get home," Lisa tells me.

"Where's home?" I ask, afraid to find out.

"North Carolina."

I can't help but smile. Their captors' route becomes semi-clear in my head: They began in Louisiana, headed east to Florida and got Paula, headed north through the Carolinas and picked up Lisa, and had since veered west to our current position in Pennsylvania. The dark-skinned girl's story is missing. I turn to her and ask what her name is.

"Gina."

"Where you from?"

"Gina."

"She doesn't speak English," Lisa informs me.

Thank God for that. I had thought she was extra traumatized.

"Do you know where they got her?" I ask.

"No. She was on the bus before me and Paula."

Upon hearing her name, Paula joins the rest of us near the shoulder. I say to Lisa, "It's almost six hours to the end. You'll never get down to North Carolina."

Lisa's eyes are trembling. They squeeze out moisture with each little shake. I feel like saying I'm sorry, but I know it'll sound hollow.

Lisa says, "I can try," and starts moving toward the bus.

"Wait wait wait," I say, following her toward the door, "the bus is mine."

"Fuck you," Lisa says, "the bus was theirs." She points to the woods. "What's wrong with your car?"

"It's out of gas."

Lisa ignores me. The back of her head seems to stick out a tongue.

"With all due respect," I say, "I just saved you."

She stops near the door and turns to face me. "Yeah, so? What good is my freedom if I can't use it?"

"I'm not the one who's stopping you from using it. It's physically impossible to drive to North Carolina before sundown."

"Not the way I drive."

"Yes, even the way *you* drive."

I hear Paula's voice right behind me. The other two have joined us near the door. "Lisa, he's got a point."

"What's his point? That he's a selfish prick?"

My chest sinks. "Who's being selfish?" I ask Lisa.

Paula plays the role of diplomat: "Look, we all have places we would like to go. I should be in Florida with my kids right now . . ."

A shiver nearly breaks me. Paula's a mom.

". . . but I know that's impossible, so I think my best bet is to get to a phone and call them. Same with you." She's referring to both Lisa and Gina. Paula looks at me: "Where were you headed?"

It's tempting to lie and say I'm going to see my wife (which would up the ante), but it's too late and hot out for bullshit. "I'm going to see the girl I love."

I expect this news to make an impact, but nobody seems to care.

Lisa says to Paula, "I won't allow him to do that. If I have to do a phone call, then he does, too."

"I'm right here. You can talk to me," I say.

The woods and grass and sky disappear. Lisa is right in my face. She hasn't brushed her teeth in quite some time. "The bus goes no further than a payphone."

I'm screaming once again. Just like at Uncle Joey's. "Why? So you can punish me? So it's fair? My fucking stop is less than three hours away! I'm the only one with a chance!"

Four long fingernails hook into my forehead and grind down my face. Blood tickles my tongue. My fist connects with soft flesh: Lisa's belly. Lisa grunts and snaps her knee up into my balls. Hot grass touches my back. Everything twirls.

I look up to see Paula training my dad's gun on Lisa. "Don't go this way, Lisa."

"Try and stop me."

Lisa steps aboard the bus. Her ass crunches as she walks, somehow mocking us. Paula looks down at me. She seems to want moral guidance. She cocks the pistol, aims it through the door.

"Don't!" I say, jumping to my feet.

The bus's engine grinds to life. I fly up the steps and inside. My hands wrap around Lisa's neck. Her long nails hook into my balls. Clear liquid squirts from my throat. Half spit, half puke. Taste of blueberries. She pulls my balls down, stretches them as far as they'll go. Black electricity snaps through me. Lisa yanks the gear into drive, kicks me in the chest with her bare heel. As the bus starts moving, I tumble down the steps and out the door.

I am the very first male to be thrown off the white bus.

17.

Paula shoots a bullet into the white bus as it sails down the freeway. I grab the gun from her and tell her not to waste the bullets. The weapon is so hot that I drop it.

I then throw my first certified *fit* since grade school. I flail my arms and legs around like they're made of rubber. Every curse ever conceived sprays from my lips. It's a rich, epic medley. Paula and Gina are sure to stand several feet away from me. Before long, my monologue rolls around to a Blame Paula speech:

"It was so nice of me to stop and pick you up! How many other people would have done that in this day and age? I fucking orchestrate your entire rescue: *my* car, *my* gun, *my* gas, *my* brains—" I jam my index fingers against my skull. "—and this is the thanks I get: being stranded out here to die on the fucking freeway!"

I desperately want Paula to defend herself. Come on, tell me how selfish I am. Get me even angrier. Make me up my hostility. Push m—

Paula's warm palms are on my shoulders. Her dried-bloody face is strangely centering. She says to me, "You did the right thing, helping us."

My face crunches up. I'm a crying little boy.

She goes on, "I know you don't believe in what you did, but it was the right thing. You gave us our last few hours back."

I point down the road and yell, "That fucking bitch took more hours than she deserved!"

Paula's hand is on my cheek. "I know," she whispers, "and I'm gonna get them back for you."

My jaw stops quivering for the first time in several minutes. Paula sounds pretty convincing for someone who's making an impossible promise. It sounds like a mom trick to me. I gotta stay on guard. "How are you gonna do that? We can't get gas anywhere."

"It's easier than you think," she whispers. "Now get your things and say goodbye to your car."

18.

This is why I avoided saying goodbye to my brother and sister. I'm standing here bidding farewell to an inanimate object (it once was animate, but not anymore), and my body is aching all over.

I tell The Horse many, many things. Private things. Things that not even I understand in their entirety. A lot of gibbering goes on. I tell him to not be scared. I'm not doing this because I don't love him, I say. I just have to move on. I'm sorry he has to be left all alone out here. I didn't plan things this way. I'm sorry he's thirsty, that I pushed him so hard. But I know that he's strong. I know that he'll still be standing here when the planet is cold and everything else has gone away.

19.

I shouldn't have spent the past six weeks watching television; my body is in no mood for exercise. We walk over two miles to the nearest exit, the one leading to the town beside mine. Maybe I'll see somebody I know. My school used to play sports against theirs.

Paula walks two steps ahead of me and Gina. The three of us bake in the sun. I imagine that the dry blood on Paula's face and scalp is very uncomfortable, not to mention the wound itself.

"Paula," I say.

"Yeah, kid?"

"I'm sorry for what I said before, about them using their pricks as weapons."

Even though I can't see Paula's face, I sense it changing. The outline of her head widens. She's smiling.

I go on, "It was the drugs."

"You should really lay off that shit."

I touch the metal bowl in my hip pocket. A zip-lock bag crinkles beneath it. It wasn't too long ago that I told Selma weed was jamming up our communication frequencies. It's tempting to empty my pocket out onto the street, but my nerves won't allow that. You never know when panic's coming.

Paula has yet to explain her game plan. I pray that she truly has one. The odds that she does are high; she hasn't lied to me yet. I play guessing games with myself until we arrive at a corner convenience store: cracked windows, no lights, open door.

"Hopefully there's water in here," Paula says, disappearing into the darkness.

Gina and I look at each other. I've never seen someone as grave looking as Gina. She's set some kind of record, even by today's standards. Her mouth brings to mind the lines on a heart monitor: mostly straight, yet twitchy and wrinkly at times. I gather that she speaks either Spanish or Italian. Too bad I slept through the former during high school.

We follow Paula into the shop. Like most stores nowadays, it's been trashed and ransacked. Most people are doing one of two things: eating like pigs or stocking up in case they survive. The reports in favor of survival predict that 60,000 of us will walk away from this thing without a scratch. I personally don't buy it, but you never know. It's interesting to think about which 60,000 might win the lottery. Hopefully there will be more women than there are men; that way they'll be able to get the whole civilization ball rolling again. (And women like Paula notwithstanding, they'll probably be more peaceful in the meantime.)

I wonder if there will be any geniuses in the new population. Mad scientists capable of drafting a new constitution or setting up a new economy. Well, even if there aren't bona fide geniuses, there will be relative geniuses. Somebody—or some group—will be recognized as intellectually superior. With any luck, that person or group will have the moral strength to get it right next time.

Paula is pouring spring water over her head. Just as I pictured it before. Her wound comes into full view; it's not as bad as I'd expected. That explains why her mind is so sharp. Don't get me wrong, though: It's still a pretty frightening gash. It looks like an eye socket after the eyeball has been torn out. My scalp tightens just from looking at it.

"Did you hit the ground with your head?" I ask her.

"I broke the fall with my hands, then my head got hit when I rolled." She stares me down. Sarcastically, she says, "But you're right: They didn't deserve to die."

My lungs release a hard chip of breath. "I never said they didn't deserve to be punished."

"Yeah? And how were we gonna do that?"

I smile. "You could have shot them between the legs."

"They would have bled to death anyway."

She's got a point there.

"Anyway," she says, "you should have thought of that then."

"Sorry, the whole heart-beating-in-my-brain thing threw me off a bit."

Paula laughs. A genuine laugh. She walks over and puts me in a loose headlock. Then she checks out my face. "You could use some water yourself."

She's referring to Lisa's scratch marks. The residue of my weed/opium high made me forget all about them. When Paula throws some water in my face, I remember them in all their stinging glory. The water is warm and silky. A little goes into my mouth and relaxes my tongue.

On our way out, we find Gina near the cash register, filling a paper bag with soda cans and packs of little fish crackers. She smiles at Paula and me, seemingly proud of her contribution. A miracle: The lady smiles. Then she gives us a little nod that I take to mean, "You guys look much better."

Paula interprets Gina's nod differently. She says to Gina, "Good question. Where to next?"

"I was wondering about that myself," I say.

We stand on the sidewalk and study the neighborhood. Standard suburbia: post office, cinema, gas station, ice cream shop. Not a soul in sight. Most of the population has been done in by fear or suicide—or both.

Paula says, "I say we knock on someone's door and ask for their car."

Every muscle in my body melts into a cozy liquid. I'm thrilled that Paula's on my side. I touch her shoulder and call her a master.

"What else did you think I had in mind?" she asks me.

"I was picturing a piggyback ride," I grin.

She pretends to punch me in the gut. I say to her, "What about your phone call?"

Paula lets out a dramatic shiver. "Not yet. That particular phone call can wait."

"Understood. What about Gina?"

"We'll make sure she gets to a phone also. Ready?"

Gina and I both nod. I admire Gina's intuition. Either she's a good performer or there's genuine perceptiveness in her eyes. I prefer to believe the latter. As we start moving to the nearest cross street, I say to Paula, "I should warn you, though: This morning I saw a man freak out over giving away a drinking glass."

Paula winks at me and says, "We're not asking for a drinking glass."

20.

We stand on the front porch of an upper-middleclass home. Paula rings the doorbell. Gina munches on fish. I tap my foot on the concrete: We've got just over five hours, and I need at least two and a half for driving.

"Nobody's home," Paula says.

"Let's try another one," I suggest, skipping off the porch without waiting for a consensus. I hear Paula and Gina land on the grass behind me. We march toward the neighbor's house. As we pass the upper-middle home's bay window, Gina lets out a scream to end all screams. Her native tongue is definitely Spanish. She's saying something about God and pointing through the dark window.

Paula makes a visor with her hand and squints through the glass. It occurs to me that Paula has bad eyesight. Maybe the bus drivers broke her glasses. Because if she could see clearly, she would have already seen the three bodies hanging from the kitchen ceiling: mother, father, and child. They used electrical cords, probably from the TV or stereo. The child looks no older than six. Chairs and stools lie sideways on the kitchen floor. The family holds hands; the child is conveniently located between the parents, unifying their souls. I'm too exhausted to be terrified. Part of me actually envies this little unit.

Paula cups her hand on the back of Gina's neck. "Don't look, come on."

Gina understands. Her eyes are red and teary as they walk on to the next house, leaving me gazing through the window. "Time is of the essence, Sean," Paula calls back to me.

I look at the slightly swaying bodies and think, *Only for some of us.*

Another porch, equally swank. Everyone around here could be dead; I'm sure the suicide rate is rising by the second. My nervous system starts accepting the idea that my day/life may end with two phone calls: one to Selma and one to home. Or at least one to Selma; I think my parents and I nailed our goodbye, so I'm hesitant to try another take. We'll see. In the meantime, nobody is answering the door.

"Is everybody gone?" Paula asks no one in particular. "Gone" sure is a pleasant way of saying "fucking dead." I don't think Paula believes these people are at the movies.

"Maybe we should shoot open a garage," I say, pleased with my ability to amend Paula's good idea with one of my own.

"*Sshhh,*" Paula goes. "I hear something."

The three of us stand at attention. (Gina of course registers the universal "*Sshhh.*") I run my palm over my face to feel if my cuts are bleeding. They're good.

Then comes the magical sound: locks clicking on the other side of the door. Unless we're about to meet a denial case, we should be on the road in no time. Come on, come on, come on.

Before my eyes compute the presence of the man in front of us, my ears hear a woman screaming somewhere inside the house. Her screams hit something deep within me; my nerves become a ball of twine. Paula hears the screaming, too (her thumb hooks into the pocket where she's holding the gun), but she puts on a natural face. The man at the door is furry and bear-like. Even though he has no facial hair, he has enough on his hands, arms, neck, and head to bring forest life to mind. Gray forest life. His face is open and innocent looking. All the more reason to believe that he has a prisoner in the back room.

"Excuse me," Paula says. "Sorry to bother you, but our car just broke down and we need to get up-state by sundown."

"Oh," the man says, his voice echoing and warm, his eyes dropping with concern, "I can't give you a ride. Sorry."

He's not closing the door, which is a good sign.

More shrieks tear their way from inside the house. Gina and I shudder. Paula remains nonchalant.

"Actually . . ." Paula says.

Let it go, I think. *There are other houses.*

". . . we were wondering if we could . . ."

I butt in, "Thanks anyway." I take Paula's free hand. Paula shakes me off and gives me a dirty look.

She continues, "We need to borrow your car."

The man's lower lip climbs inside his mouth. When he releases it, he says with an ironic smile, "You mean *take* my car."

Paula and I pretend to laugh. More high holy yells from inside the house. Paula probably thinks the screamer is merely frightened of the end. She and I rarely draw the same conclusions.

"It would mean a lot to us. And if you're not using it . . ."

The man frowns with confusion. He probably thinks we're a hallucination. He's got one hand on the inner doorknob. Then he says, "Sure, I don't see why not."

Inside my head, a gear spins and puts a smile on my face.

"But, if it doesn't bother you," the man says, "I'd like to ask for something in return."

The gear in my head spins back to its original position. This is it: the part where he asks for our kidneys in return for the car. I nearly grab the gun from Paula's overalls.

The man says, "My wife is about to give birth to our first child. She's due any second now. Would you all mind giving me some help?"

My eyes pan from the gun to the man. Pointing to herself and Gina, Paula says, "Oh of course. We can stay, but he's gotta run."

Paula's long pink thumbnail is cocked my way. The man stares me up and down. He's studying my face, which means he sees the cuts, which means—given Paula's fib about our car breaking down—he probably thinks we were in an accident. "That's no problem," he says.

I feel something rise inside of me, and I say to the man, "Whatever. I'll help out, too."

The man nods slightly, turns around, and goes back into his house.

21.

Maybe Paula thinks I'm a hypocrite for opting to stay. Maybe she thinks I was lying about being in a rush. But I can't worry about that right now: I have to see this baby come into the world.

I have to see this baby come into the world because I want to get a look at its face. (The parents don't know if it's a he or a she.) I am compelled by my very soul to look into the face of this new arrival. This odd traveler, the spirit of whom chose to arrive on Earth just as the human experiment was concluding.

They say that babies are born every minute. But, as Selma once informed me, it's actually unfair to say that they're *born*. It's more just and scientifically sound to say that they *arrive*. Because *born* is passive; it implies that the mother is squeezing out the child and that's that. The truth is that the baby climbs out. The thing doesn't snap to life when its body encounters the freezing air—no. It works hard. For hours and days. The process of labor has every bit as much to do with the mother's efforts as it does with those of the infant.

Paula of course knows this, as does every mother in the world. But it came as news to me less than six months ago. And, more than any other fact of nature, it gives me hope that there's another world.

Because if the path of an infant is active and not passive, then the same must be said for the path of the fetus, and the path of the sperm. Willpower is present at every step along the way. All forms of life are possessed of a sparkling drive.

So who is this pilgrim that's about to greet us? What business could he/she possibly have in this forsaken place? Is he/she some kind of anomaly, a cosmic accident? Fallout from an inept calculation by the gods? Or does something inside of him/her desire to be here?

While my eyes are fixed on the impossible sight of the baby's skull jutting from the aging woman's body, I think about tunnels. The artist in me goes crazy with the possibilities: I picture red tunnels, yellow ones, green, blue, purple. Triangular, circular, diamond-shaped, square. So many tunnels in life, and in the universe at large. Like the freeway less than a mile from here. That's my tunnel for today. If viewed from a distance, I'll bet that my whole life has the shape of a tunnel. And I'll bet that this tunnel extends to another realm. The journey cannot end here.

These thoughts aren't new to me. I've tinkered around with them before, but something about this living room and these screams and this couple and their baby makes me stop thinking these thoughts and start feeling them.

I need this feeling to hang on tight. We encounter so many crappy, loosely woven emotions throughout our lives. Fleeting bullshit that seems so strong and smells so fresh, only to collapse into nothingness a moment later. Very rarely do we get *branded*. I want the feeling of these tunnels to burn into my brain. I don't care if the burn is agonizing. It doesn't matter if it leaves me blind. Because right now, possibly for the first time, I see the light that humans have spoken of since history began.

History is ending. So please let me go out with faith. I've been robbed of the chance to become a whole person, so just give me this one little thing. Send me on my way with faith in my mind and in my heart. My faith doesn't have to be formal or decorative or rooted in verse: Just keep this pathway open and let the light flow in.

Paula sees the change in my expression. She takes her eye away from the video camera's viewfinder. The man asked her to tape the event. When she asked him why—considering there wasn't much time to watch it, blah blah blah—he said that maybe people (or other beings) will visit his home someday and take a look at the recording. Maybe they'll be able to learn a little something about the history of our barren world. I personally suspect that the tape will turn into dust before anybody ever watches it, but then again: Anything's possible. If the sight of a little bald head emerging from a woman's vagina teaches us anything, it's that anything – is – possible.

Something resembling cynicism tickles my thoughts. It tells me that I'm being a freak, that I should stop with all the bullshit already because nobody really knows anything, now do they? True enough, the light whispers back. But you don't have to know to believe.

A sixth person has entered the room. While Paula runs the camera, Gina dips a wet cloth into a mixing bowl, and Mrs. Perkins wheezes, Mr. Perkins holds up their new daughter. He lifts her as high as she'll go. I take a close look at that face. She's incredibly stunning for someone who's so sticky and discolored. After some maneuvers involving gauze and barber's sheers, Mr. Perkins snips his daughter's umbilical cord. There's no turning back now, kid. You've abandoned your safety rope.

Gina's eyes are ready to depart from her skull. They're so wide that I could iron my shirt on them. Paula's face, which was blood red when I met her, has now gone pink. Her eyes wring out some serious moisture. Tears dangle from her chin before free-falling to the carpet. Mr. Perkins hands Mrs. Perkins their child. The infant Perkins produces screams that outdo anything I've heard all day.

I just stand there and smile. It's not a tight smile that hurts my face, just a subtle flex of joy. A spacious moment passes before common sense breaks up my reverie.

Time to hit the road.

22.

Paula and Gina opt to stay put. (The latter doesn't really *opt*, but the conventional wisdom is that she should do whatever Paula does. Neither of them have any more business to conduct with me.) Paula's plan is to retreat into the bedroom and call her husband and kids. She hopes to be on with them up until the end. Mr. Perkins says he has a basement line that Gina can use. The word *telefono* works wonders at getting the message across.

I stand in the hallway outside the Perkins' living room and look into Paula's eyes. We're close enough to kiss, but I doubt that will happen. This unusual woman, who I've known for half an afternoon but feel very close to, graces me with a classic smile. It sends musical notes up and down my body. "There's something freeing about all this, isn't there?" she says.

"Yeah, kind of. But I think the older you are, the more free you feel. I wouldn't have minded getting a little older."

"Your soul seems pretty old."

"I thought you didn't believe in that bullshit."

"You never know."

"We could know pretty soon."

Her arms wrap around me. This hug is beyond measurement. It contains corridors and balconies and secret passageways. I could very easily get lost in it. But I have to make myself step away. Paula says to me, "Sorry I got you caught up in all that shit."

"Please. That's crazy. I'm glad that you're here and not out there on the freeway."

Paula nods. "Speaking of which . . ."

"Yeah." I jiggle the keys in my hand. "Thanks for the car. See you later."

"See you."

I kiss Paula on the cheek.

As I open the door to the garage, Mr. Perkins calls out to me: "Hey Sean, we're taking a survey. What do you think we should call this little beauty?"

I turn toward the living room and lock eyes with the old man. "How 'bout Selma?" I suggest.

Mr. Perkins folds his lips downward and nods. "Not bad, not bad."

I step into the garage and check out the Perkins' silver Dodge Shadow. Its hood gives me a respectful nod. I stop moving again. "Hey Mr. Perkins," I call out, "do you have a nickname for your car?"

Mr. Perkins lets out a hearty laugh. "No, we never gave her one. Any ideas?"

"I don't know," I say, picturing silver bullets. "She looks kind of like a Wolf if you ask me."

23.

If men and women were to exist in a few hundred years, and if they were to take pen to paper and write of legendary things, I expect that they would write about me and The Wolf. I expect that they would write about me and The Wolf as we blazed across my state, bonding faster than we drove, breaking every speed barrier known to man.

Leave it to Mr. Perkins—a man who's inclined to videotape his child's birth on the world's last day—to have a full tank of gas in his car. The fuel intoxicates The Wolf's awesome mind, and her tires hover just above the ground. As the sun loses its brutal edge, it plays gently off of the trees at our sides, making them twinkle and glow. The near-perfect alignment of the trees keeps my faith intact. As The Wolf glides past them, I imagine that my eyes are guitar picks and the trees are an infinite arrangement of strings. (This fancy will have to do because the radio gets no reception out here.)

Before long, we clear the trees and are in the midst of hills. Their emerald grass blades sing glittery notes. My mouth hangs open, inhaling the scenery. And my brain reclines comfortably within my skull. I feel that my thoughts are safe from panic. I'm a little ragged, a little exhausted, but my essence flows like water from a pitcher. I'm no longer dry inside; I'm good and moist. Zero percent humidity. For that force we call God is in these hills, just as It was in those trees, just as It lines the machinery within The Wolf. Everything swells with Its soothing might. I always knew It was there, but I've never seen or felt It up till now.

The infant Perkins (whom I prefer to call "Selma" in my mind) had some mug on her. Her eyes weren't dim or shallow; they were bright and deep. Some grueling mission she selected. Though I can't quite be sure why she's here, I know it has something to do with her parents. Accompanying them through their hardest hours, giving them a taste of happiness. And though it may sound egotistical, I suspect that her mission has a little something to do with me. Because it's not just The Wolf and me out here. Baby Selma is in our hearts. The road I'm now on began with one Selma and shall end with another.

Still, in the cellar of my mind, I feel a little dread. No, that's incorrect. I feel no dread; I just logically understand that dread is possible. This could very well be a mania state designed by my unconscious to counter my previous depressed/anxious state. Well, if that's the case, so be it. I just hope to go out on a high.

"You're gonna die, Sean," I tell myself, well aware of how hokey it sounds, yet equally aware that the statement is no less true for being hokey.

The fact that we will all die is so obvious, so known, so recorded, such a given, that it was almost boring six weeks ago. We spoke of our impending demises with resolved indifference. Shrugged our shoulders and said, "Yeah, I'd like to own a boat someday . . . or open a restaurant someday . . . or call that girl back someday . . . or adopt a kid someday . . . or learn the piano someday . . . *assuming that I don't die before then.*"

Maybe the Almighty got sick of that mindset. Perhaps It wanted to shake us all up a bit by giving the concept of death a nice, aggressive polish, then presenting it anew so we would all jump and stir. It's very stimulating, the knowledge that we'll die. If we think about it enough, it makes us more assertive, pushes us to get more done, makes us value our time more. Or at least some of us. Others, when forced to consider dying, consider it all the way to the point of action: They take their own lives. So thinking about death either pushes you more toward death or more toward life. I'm lucky to be experiencing the latter push. In many ways, I've just begun feeling alive.

Happy Birthday to me and Baby Selma! Which begs the question: If her mission was to enliven her parents and show me the tunnels, then what is my mission? I used to think my mission was to draw and paint, but I could never let myself fully believe that. Too pretentious and obvious. Don't get me wrong: People have always enjoyed my work. But there has to be more to life than just stimulating people. One must go beyond stimulation and truly participate.

Have I participated? When Baby Selma was born, I was merely a witness. When Paula took vengeance, I was merely a driver cum idea man. When my Circle mates confessed this morning, I barely listened. When Uncle Joey gave me free food and drink, I thanked him by losing my temper. When I left the house, I avoided my siblings. I've always put myself first, and in so doing, I've been completely closed off to any possible mission that I may have.

Even my goal of fucking Selma is unreasonably self-serving. Why do I even think of it as *fucking*? Why have I never come around to the idea of making love? Am I incapable of sharing?

My tunnel to the beyond is closing. Its light grows dim.

Shit! Don't do this to yourself. You were doing so well. Come on, picture the tunnels. All different colors. Fuck, no colors; only gray and brown. Even the grass looks gray and brown. I'm an asshole. I need to smoke. My pipe, lighter, and weed are riding shotgun. I blanket them with my hand. Then I realize what was in Baby Selma's eyes. Not just light and depth, but judgment. She was deconstructing me in her mind. Part of her probably wondered why I hadn't helped with her birth. Within her tiny head were oceans of wisdom, fresh from the other realm. And within those oceans was the knowledge that I'm not whole.

Maybe I haven't been born yet. Maybe I've just entered the birth canal.

I grab my pipe, light, and bag with my right hand and roll down my window with my left. The items *clink* as they hit the pavement. Grow the fuck up already, Sean. Reality is headed my way, so I best not keep hiding from it.

The thought camps out in my every cell: Reality is headed my way.

Reality and a large tan Buick.

24.

Whatever they injected me with, it was some serious shit. My brain is out for a swim. The room is small, so small that it's in the running to be a closet. Steel walls, steel floor, steel ceiling, steel table, all of it shined to a fever pitch: silver reflecting silver reflecting silver. The man before me has a tense face. I bet that if I were to peel his skin off, his skeleton would be made of more steel. He smiles and his teeth shine. Are they white or silver behind that shine?

"Don't worry Sean . . ."

"Don't worry Sean . . ."

Everything he says has an echo. Only it's not an echo, because the second version is always as crisp as the first. I grab onto my knees—my bare knees. I'm naked. My ass is kissing the steel chair beneath me, penis hanging like a deflated balloon.

"We're not your enemies . . ."

"We're not your enemies . . ."

Enemies? Christ! Who said anything about enemies? I don't trust this man. Getting up and leaving seems necessary, but there's no door in here.

"We're here to help . . ."

"We're here to help . . ."

Maybe there's a secret passageway. I always wanted to go through one of those. Is there a lever or a switch or—?

"You're sick . . . your mind isn't well . . ."

"You're sick . . . your mind isn't well . . ."

His voice isn't right. I bet his vocal cords are made of steel, too. Curled silver wires. He must need oil to clear his throat.

"We're licensed doctors . . ."

"We're licensed doctors . . ."

Who's "we," anyway? There's only one of him. Repeating voice, yes, but only one regardless. My tongue wiggles; I'd like to speak. It briefly sticks to the roof of my mouth, then flicks the rears of my upper teeth. I say, "Who's 'we'?"

The steel man pauses. His eyes become tinted glass. He replies, "Me and the man in the corner."

"Me and the man in the corner."

The corner.

I turn around. Since the room is round (or ovoid?), there is no corner, but seated on the floor, leaning against the wall, is a second man. This one has deep red skin and no hair. His suit—gray, clean, efficient—matches that of the steel man across from me. His eyes are as red as his skin, but their moistness gives them away. He smiles: red gums, dark pink teeth. Teeth shining like the walls, floor, ceiling, and table. Back to the table. The steel man now has a notepad. White paper, no lines on it. Silver steel pen, serrated tip. Slashing the paper. Notes. He's writing down things about me.

I should be afraid, but the chemicals have driven a wedge between myself and my experiences. I say, "Are you gonna ask me questions?"

"Is that okay with you?"

"Is that okay with you?"

"Depends on the questions."

"Okay . . ."

"Okay . . ."

(My heart is erupting.)

"We'll start off easily . . ."

". . . easily, easily . . ."

Then the man is standing. I like his shoes. Hard and tight. The laces seem looped through his very feet.

Before I know it, he's not echoing, or whatever it was. He's still got a wiry voice, though: "Do you know why you're here?"

I nod. No bones in my neck. "You were in the Buick. You took me from my Wolf."

The man's laughter sends my eardrums through a shredder. "That doesn't really settle the question of *why*, now does it, Sean?"

The chemicals dissipate. Everything surges toward me. Thickness and clarity. Too much clarity. I can't blink. My peripheral vision splits wide open. I could dip my fingertips in my pupils.

The steel man's question answers itself. Or rather, the pale glow of my face answers it. I can see my face on the opposite wall. It's flattened, ready to crack. The steel man is seated again.

"You're here because this is a *psychiatric facility*. . ." He gives the last two words condescending emphasis. He may as well be saying *kindergarten*.

"Your mother and father brought you in here because you were having some intense delusions. But we've given you something to make you slow down."

That's funny, 'cuz I'm moving real fast. Thoughts whiz forward with so much momentum that they don't have time to stop and reveal themselves.

"You thought the world was ending, Sean."
"You thought the world was ending, Sean."
"You stole a gun from your father and left your house."
"Stole a gun, left your house."
"You stole a car from a man and were driving north."
"Car, man, north."
"You, you, you."
"You, you, you."

I'm on my feet. My naked body looks crooked on the opposite wall. The steel man looks at my penis and his lower jaw drops slightly. I manage to catch a thought and catapult it from my throat: "Bullshit. I can explain."

The red man now licks my back.

I can't turn around. What if he bites me?

"You've already explained."
"Already."
"You've told us about Selma."
"Selma."
"And Paula."
"Paula."
"Lisa."
"Lisa."
"Gina."
"Gina."

My eyelids are droopy. Behind them are crackles of tenderness. The red man has lumps on his tongue. Diagonal slashes of saliva begin to drip down my back.

The steel man is in my face, close enough to lick me himself. His breath smells like a handful of fresh gears and screws. He says, "We have your whole story, Sean. And we'd like to patiently explain that it's not possible."

"Possible."
"Patient."
"Possible."

Blood charges through my head, but I'm still listening. He goes on:

"It's what we call an unintended structural pattern. When a schizophrenic involuntarily applies form to his or her hallucinations."

The red man stops licking, merely breathes.

Steel man sits down, says, "All the women you say you met had names ending with the letter *a*. That's not possible."

My lips move, producing nothing. My saliva ducts pop, keel over, die.

"Would you like to sit down?"
"Would you like to sit down?"

I sit. The red man is already in the chair. His lap is warm.

"We gave you the drugs so you would understand."
"We gave you the drugs so you would understand."

"Do you?"
"Do you?"
"Understand?"

They probably stripped me of my clothes so I wouldn't use them to choke myself. The least they could've given me was a paper gown. Maybe if I rub my wrists hard against the steel tabletop, they'll chafe and eventually open.

"I know it's a lot to handle."
"A lot to handle."
"But we can help you."
"You you."

I need my mother. Everything is slanted. There's no way out of this wilderness. The red man's thighs are stirring. Soon he'll be excited.

The steel man's eyes are magnetic; he uses them to attract my own eyes. We stare into each other. He asks me if I think he makes sense.

"Do you think?"

"Do you think?"

Ever since I was a little kid, I always worried my brain would go. My teachers called me creative, but I knew something malicious was at work. Some fiendish demon was slowly chewing through my skull. Thank God I never made it to Selma's. How could I explain this to her?

One red hand curls around me, strokes my pounding chest.

Atop the smooth red thumb lies Baby Selma. A miniature version of Baby Selma, sucking on her own microscopic fingers. She looks up at me and says, "Sean, my mommy's name doesn't end with *a*."

I look at the steel man and say, "Mrs. Perkins."

He frowns. Bolts bend inside of him.

Baby Selma goes on, "Her name was Janice."

"Her name was Janice," I repeat.

The steel man rises from his chair.

Then I come around on the grass and feel two chubby palms slapping my cheeks. A man and a woman, both very roundish, stand above me. The man wears a stained fedora. I sit up fast, fast enough to scare them. They run a few steps away, then slowly approach me again. Their breath is forced, wheezy.

"You're okay," the man says, unsure whether to cap that off with a question mark.

I answer him regardless: "I'm okay."

I look to my right. The Wolf stands nobly on the freeway. Her left headlight has been bashed to pieces, but otherwise she's looking strong. The Buick's left headlight has the same injury.

"We were driving the wrong way," the woman explains, sounding disappointed in herself.

"This guy was after us," says the man.

"From the circus," the woman goes.

My whole body creaks as I climb to my feet. "Is there anything wrong with me?" I ask the man, fearing that I have a steering column lodged in my neck.

"I think you're fine."

The woman nods rapidly.

The man continues, "After the accident, you ran out of your car and screamed something about wolves. Then you fainted, I guess."

"'The Wolf can't be gone,' it was," the woman helpfully quotes.

I look from the woman to the man and then back again.

"Well, she's not," I smile.

Black dots float before me.

"Look, we're so sorry," says the woman.

"Yeah," adds the man. "Gosh, to think that we almost ended up taking a life with only two hours till the end."

"Two hours," I say, not to them as much as to myself, not to mention The Wolf. My eyes trace dark pavement as I approach my vehicle. The door stands courteously open.

Before I get in, I take one last look at the heavy woman.

"Excuse me," I say. "What's your name?"

"Me? Susan."

"Susan? . . . Is that short for Susanna or something?"

She takes a step backward as she shakes her head.

"Good," I grin.

Then I take a seat and go.

25.

I knew little about Brian before Selma fucked him. He was just a face around campus. Dark blonde hair, round jaw, admittedly cute. Vague, average, nothing special. Everybody seemed to like him. But when he became my enemy, I became an expert on the topic of Brian.

Transfer student from Illinois (fucking out-of-state punk). In his third year (stupid young little baby). Dated this Italian girl named Connie for a long time (can't find fault with that). Pledged some fraternities but backed out because he thought it was bullshit (I wish he had stayed aboard; would've been one more reason to hate him). Had the *Die Hard* trilogy on video in his dorm room (fucking shallow prick). Always ate salad in the dining hall (pussy). Wore a silver ring on his thumb (pretentious scum).

Before Selma took it upon herself to remove her clothes and underclothes and let Brian become the second person to penetrate her body, I was half-aware that they knew each other. I vaguely recall Brian cornering her in the dining hall and muttering something about Movie Night in the student center. I also recall Selma smiling, but that could be imaginative license. In any case, whenever the seeds were planted, they sure ended up growing. Tall. Into thick, sharp weeds of despair. The situation was so ugly that it even got me thinking in gardening metaphors.

Her version: "I'm so sorry, Sean. You have every reason to hate me. I'm so stupid for drinking that much. I wasn't myself. It meant nothing. I love you so much. I'm so afraid of losing you."

His version: "Hey, man." (Said to me in passing on a sunny spring day in the park. His gleaming smile would have looked nice with a golf club slammed through it.)

My take: "Selma, if it meant nothing, then I must mean nothing, right? I must mean *absolutely nothing!*"

I was more of an existentialist back in those days.

We stopped talking. Less than a month to go before graduation. She left me voicemails, wrote messages on my dry-erase board. I retreated into the thicket of my anger. Walked around sneering. Frowned my way through finals. Made out with this girl Rachel at some boring party. (The make-out session did little to alleviate the boredom.) I bitched to my friends about how bad the love hurt, how all I wanted was to shake the love out of my system. "It never goes away," we all agreed.

I told my mother the whole sordid story. She had met Selma several times; on move-in days, move-out days, during winter and summer breaks. The two of them had liked each other. But not anymore. After the incident, my mother freely referred to her as a little slut. She even claimed to have had Selma's number from the beginning: "She was too loose, that one," Mom would say. "She shouldn't have been kissing you in front of your mother."

I wanted to agree. When Mom tore into Selma, I wanted to become all juiced-up with dark adrenaline. High on my own sense of justice: "Fuck Selma," I wanted to say and think. "Just a useless, dirty slut."

But I couldn't get into it. My head was packed with too many heightened, blissful memories.

Every year, Selma got the flu. One year, she was in bed for a week. I was *so* attracted to her while she was in that state: tired, drowsy, dizzy, delirious. Babbling incoherently. Groaning with discomfort. It was the most adorable thing I've ever seen. I couldn't stay away from her. We fucked in her bed, and within the week I was blowing my nose and drinking orange juice. And you know what?

It was worth it.

Selma, Selma, Selma. Where did she come from? What the hell kind of magic had she worked on me?

Two days before graduation, I was drunk in my room. Wandering around and sipping from a silver flask was key to my despair phase. I preferred brandy, but anything hard did the trick. Anyway, I was shit-faced and talking to the mirror. Trying to figure out what the hell was behind all that hard bone and tight flesh. Tapping my reflection with my fingertip, leaving smudges on the glass. Despising all human life, myself very much included. Before long, I stuck my flask down the front of my jeans and stomped into the hallway. I kept my head down; didn't want anyone knowing I was fucked up. (In hindsight, it was probably obvious. If I remember correctly, I was muttering curses to myself.)

I walked down two flights of stairs to Selma's floor. Pounded on her door hard enough to leave dents. Scribbled nonsense all over her dry-erase board while waiting for her to answer. When she did so, she smiled. A layer of moisture gave a shine to her eyes. (I remember reading somewhere that if a girl's eyes are moist when she looks at you, it means that she's attracted to you. The subtle tear-duct activity is indicative of low-grade emotion. The same of course goes for guys' eyes.)

"Sean," she said, "I'm so sorry. I can't even tell you."

I shoved past her and sat on her bed, said, "Oh, I think you can tell me."

Selma knelt before me. "I would do anything to make this right."

"It's all wrong, Selma. All wrong."

That's when she realized I was drunk. She put her hand on my knee. I became turned on and loathed myself. Her mint breath touched me. I stood up and paced, concealing my hard-on by putting my hands in my pockets and opening them wide.

"What is it about me, Selma?"

"It wasn't you."

"Yeah, yeah, yeah. You can say that, but at some subconscious level: This Is About Me." I pointed at my chest like Tom Cruise did during monologues. (I truly wish I'd spent my life living rather than watching movies.)

Selma stood and touched my wrists. She tried to remove my hands from my pockets, but that was inadmissible. She settled for removing the flask from my pants and placing it on her desk. Her manner brought to mind a teacher removing a slingshot from a student's hands: "I'll have this."

"Tell me, Selma. I'm not leaving till you do."

The truth is, I really did feel like leaving. I had a swelling urge to run back up to my room and angrily undo my erection. But, in the interest of being a man of my word, I stood right there.

Selma bit her lower lip. "I'm not gonna make something up, Sean."

"That's good to know. 'Cause I want the truth."

"I love you."

"But you want to fuck Brian."

"I don't want to do that."

"Oh, sorry. Correction: You *wanted* to."

"I was drunk. Just like you are now."

"Wow. Yay! Nice job, Selma. You Political Science majors really know how to argue don't you? Well, you happen to be right. I am drunk. But you know what? Guess what? My fucking clothes are still on!"

"*Ssshh!* People can probably hear."

"Good! Thank God. At least someone's listening. You never did."

"What's that supposed to mean?"

I had no clue what that was supposed to mean, so I veered the conversation back on course: "A reason, Selma. If you say you didn't have a *motive*, then fine, I believe you. So just come up with a reason. There must be something so inherently terrible and disgusting about me that you would piss away two years of a relationship."

"Shut up. I don't like that. 'Piss away.'"

"Oh, right. Sorry. You don't like piss. Only come. Brian's come, my come. Whatever you can get your mouth on."

There were hands in my face at that point. Slapping me, pinching me, trying to tear my eyebrows off. Selma was growling; her teeth were actually bare. Amid the slaps and growls, I caught her answer: "Because you're a self-absorbed egomaniac, okay? Everyone knows that."

I passed by Selma at graduation. She smiled and said, "Congratulations." Her arms were horizontal. I told her to go to hell and kept on walking.

26.

Shortly after I take the exit to Selma's neighborhood, I hear something crunch beneath The Wolf's front left tire. I hit a rabbit once back in high school, and this crunch sounds an awful lot like that one. The Wolf and I ask each other, "What was that?"

Curiosity is a bitch. Morbid curiosity is an even nastier bitch. The sun is dropping and civilization is crumbling, yet I'm pulling over to see what the hell I've hit. The Wolf wishes me luck as I step outside. "Don't worry about me," I tell her. Seeing as I've handled human corpses recently, I don't think the sight of a dead squirrel or bunny will do me in.

My guts do a little dance. I puke warm soda all over the ground, charring the back of my throat.

It's a little hand. Dark, cracked, flattened against the road. Looks like it belonged to a female. Hundreds of ants have a field day with it. I expect a one-handed woman to leap from the woods. I'm back inside The Wolf before the image fully materializes.

"Let's go, Wolfie."
She kicks into gear.
"What did you find, Sean?"
"Something not good."

27.

I'm 99 percent sure that that hand didn't belong to Selma. After all, I'm closely acquainted with Selma's hands. I've had them on my face, in my mouth, around my manhood. The hand I saw was smaller than Selmas' (not to mention flatter). It also had shorter fingernails (unless Selma cut hers recently, but that's doubtful; she's too feminine). Despite my relative certainty, I pull over at the gas station payphone ten blocks from Selma's house. This choice will go down as the worst one I ever made.

Something's wrong with the air. I can't put my finger on it. I'm not sure if I smell something, or if the temperature's weird, or . . . I . . . don't . . . know. Maybe the approaching rock is messing with the Earth's field of gravity. But none of the news reports said anything about that, and I know absolutely nothing about astronomy, so that theory isn't worth mulling over. Perhaps my nerves are just fucked and my perception is off. Anything's possible. I stick a quarter in the slot and dial Selma's number.

Selma is screaming:

"Sean?"

"Yeah. Selma?"

"Are you okay?"

"Yeah. I'm—"

"You took forever. Where are you?"

"I'm at the gas station near your—"

"Sean! Get over here now!"

"What's the—?"

"You're on a payphone?"

"Y—"

"Shit! Get in your car and come straight here."

"What is it? Are you okay?"

"Yeah, *we're* okay. We've got walls around us. Get the fuck in your car this second."

"I—"

"Now! Don't think! Now!"

Selma slams her phone down.

I hear a crack somewhere behind me. My hands shake so badly that I can't return the phone to its cradle. It drops, bungees, and swings like a pendulum. The payphone's blurred steel gives me no useful reflections.

I wish The Wolf would say what's behind me.

Another loud crack. This one sharper.

I look over my shoulder. Behind me, strolling along the sidewalk some fifty feet away, is a man with a curly black mustache and tidy black hair. His bright smile punches a hole through the dusk. He wears a loud red jacket and drags a snaky whip.

For some foolish reason, my brain plays the rhythm of a poem I wrote back in grade school. I can't quite piece the words together, but if I could they'd go like this:

There was a really scary man,
With a scary monster face.
And when I saw that scary man,
My heart began to race.

But it's not really the man who's scary. It's the two giant cats walking alongside him. I believe *lions* is the technical term.

He *smashes* his leather whip against the ground.

28.

Lions lick chops.
Red-stained beards. Pink teeth.
Whip *cracks*.
Lions run at me.
I run at Wolf.
(Wolf cries.)
Lions run.
I run.
Lions.

Me.
Lions.
Me.
Sneakers untied. Sweaty face.
Sun dropping.
Lions.
Me.
Lions.
Fast.
Muscle.
Manes.
Blood drips.
Whip.
Sun drops.
(Man in red.)
I'm in The Wolf. Vinyl beneath me. Keys in wet hand. Aim at ignition.
Growls.
Lion's snout sticks through my door.
Close it! Close!
Growling.
Nostril breath on me.
(Baby Selma stares.)
Closing-door-with-all-my-might.
Whip cracks, hisses.
"Fuck!"
Lion's face close. In closing door. Nose tickles me.
Tongue.
Tongue.
Tongue.
Rat-a-tat-tat: my heart.
Saliva on me.
Other lion licks passenger window. *Crashes* head through window.
Key not in slot.

Hand of stone.
(Wolf's last words: "Move now!")
Key slides.
Left lion licks thigh.
Holding door with adrenal reserves.
Lions' eyes shine.
Right lion licks ear.
Foot on gas.
Red jacket in rearview.
Pedal on carpet.
Tires squeal-spin.
Two lions fall down.
Driver's door shut.
And then I'm gone.

29.

The Wolf has never run so fast. She cannot bear to speak. That's just as well; my own innards have hardened and I wouldn't be able to reply. We roar (Don't think about roaring.) toward Selma's house. Less than eight blocks. Keep your eye on the prize. Maybe you were only dreaming.

Go, go.

I feel the lion's spit on my jeans and know I was awake.

Go, go, go.

This is what happens near the end. Civilization descends to the rules of the jungle. And we all know who's king of the jungle. Via one trainer's madness, these lions have emerged to reclaim the throne.

Go, go, go, go.

Selma's town looks different. I've seen these trees and houses and porches and lawns and swing-sets and baby pools a million times before, but never with a veil of doom over them. Everything is gray, and I can't find a glow or a shine.

We hang a sharp right, then go *crunch.*

The windshield shatters.

Beige hair fills my sight. Short beige hair, no mane. The lion we hit is a female.

Its back gets sliced on the windshield. It lets out a sad, anguished bark. The Wolf goes into a spin. No more road beneath us. Something softer. Grass. My jaw hits the top rim of the steering wheel when we stop.

How many lions are there? My mind splits open. I envision lions in my trunk. Lions in my backseat. Lions on my lap. Lion DNA in my body.

I exit The Wolf, don't bother to look at the beast on my hood. According to my peripheral vision, she's a dead slab of hair. I leave one of my shoes behind as I run across an anonymous front lawn. Up the porch steps. Grip the handle. Front door open. Step inside. Spin lock behind me.

Lots of chatter in the kitchen. Fervor. Passion. Declaration. Debate.

I see a lion traipsing down the staircase. Two blinks make it vanish.

From the kitchen, a man's voice: "I'm telling you, Larry, I've done research. It's all *right here.*"

I hear pages turning. A book hitting a tabletop.

Another man, presumably Larry, says, "I know you have, Joel. But I still think we should stay behind closed doors. It's not worth it."

Joel comes back with, "Of course it's worth it. Didn't you ever want to do anything with your life?"

"I already have," says Larry.

Lots of chatter. Fifteen, sixteen voices. Men, women. I hear bustling on the stovetop: pots, pans, sizzling, broiling.

I make my way toward the kitchen. Its light is the only one visible.

Joel says, "We've got the backyard covered in gasoline. All we need is one of two things: a dead lion or a great deal of human blood."

An uproar of chatter. I step into the kitchen expecting to see a session of Parliament. Instead, I see over a dozen senior citizens, barking at each other in a haze of cigar smoke. The men have their shirtsleeves rolled up. The women rest their chins on their palms. Eyes roll and tongues click.

Larry speaks again, and I pick him out: dyed black hair, frowning lips, a plump nose you wanna reach out and squeeze. "I'd rather be killed by a meteorite than in the jaws of a lion. But that's just me."

A woman with too much lipstick chimes in, "I don't understand you men. Right up till the end, you're bickering and bullshitting. Who cares about the dumb lions? We should all be talking about God right now."

I can't decide which is more shocking: the animals in the street or the scholars in this kitchen. They're ostensibly having the same debate Paula and I had, pitting forceful resistance against peaceful resistance. I don't much care for the lipstick woman's male stereotyping. Somebody should tell her what cowards we are.

A tiny gentleman rises from his seat. His hair is white and compact, his face taut from plastic surgery. I've never seen eyes as blue as his. This can only be Joel. When he speaks, he confirms my guess. He stares down the lipstick woman and says, "Katherine,

I've never stopped being a man since I was fourteen, and I don't intend to stop now."

A shot goes through me. Fourteen? The only thing I cared about at that age was who I'd invite to sleep over on Friday night.

Katherine shakes her head. "I don't see anything manly about fighting wild animals. It's silly is what it is."

Joel slams his palm down on the kitchen table and says, "On pure principle, Katherine, I will not allow some nutcase to terrorize us just because our time is up. To allow that would be to let go of my humanity, just like all those goddamn suicides!"

That line gets lots of nods. Few among the living respect the suicides.

Joel clears his throat and goes on, "Now, according to this book," he taps the glossy page of an encyclopedia, "they're drawn to the scent of either *blood* or *each other*. So we either get a lion corpse in the backyard or start cutting ourselves open." Joel rolls up his sleeves as high as they'll go. "I for one am prepared to do either."

The room ignites with talk.

"You've lost it, Joel," a fat man says.

"I would feel comfortable if we all just prayed," Katherine laments.

Two women whisper to each other and giggle. A man with messy hair shuffles a deck of cards and begins a game of solitaire. Larry gets up and exits, presumably to use the bathroom.

Scratch what I said about male cowardice. Joel somehow got to me. Though I only half-trust the feeling, something in my gut is telling me it's time to use force.

"Excuse me," I say.

Nobody hears or sees me. I clear my throat:

"Excuse me!"

Silence. All eyes on me. Just like the Meditation Circle. I must be some sight to see: scratched face, bloodshot eyes, spit-drenched pant leg, twitching appendages.

I say to the room, "I've got a dead lion outside on the hood of my car."

Joel aims his baby blues at me. He's too focused on his goal to wonder what I'm doing here. He smiles and says, "Thank you, son."

30.

Less than sixty minutes to the fall. I volunteer to help carry the dead lion to the backyard. They've got the yard doused in gasoline, so the plan is to plant the dead animal on the grass, wait for its friends (three of them altogether, according to Larry), and then throw a lit match on the lawn. Goodbye lions. While Joel, Larry, and I pace toward the front door, I ask them if the tamer can prevent the lions from entering the trap. They assure me that the tamer won't know it's a trap.

"I can't believe I'm going through with this," Larry says to Joel.

"Stop complaining. Would you rather be on your knees waiting to die?" Joel says to Larry. "Be a mensch."

Joel opens the front door. The Wolf lies broken on the grass. The mane-less cat is right where I left her two minutes ago. Part of me feels bad for her, but the other nine-tenths of me is pleased.

We move quickly. Joel and Larry step to opposite sides of the animal. I guess that leaves me with
the middle.

"We're gonna get bloody," says Joel, lifting the
corpse, "so we'll toss our clothes in the back, too."

"Good idea," Larry groans, lifting his end.

I step to the center and hook my arms under
the lion's ribcage.

Then Joel snorts. Or was that Larry?

The lion's face is in mine. I see its teeth and
throat. Its roar burns my cuts.

We drop the lion and run toward the porch.
The animal lands on its feet. It shakes its body the way
a dog does after a bath. Blood sprays on the door as
we slam it.

31.

The books and plates have been cleared off the
kitchen table. Joel, Larry, and I throw our bloody
clothes on its center. We stand in our underwear: Joel
and Larry wear boxers and T-shirts; I wear only
boxers. I feel Katherine eyeing my torso, and I cross
my arms. Joel shakes his head and says, "It's not
enough. We need *lots* of blood."

"Cut me," I say. No contemplation.

Joel shares my enthusiasm for time manage-
ment. Without a nod or a glance, he moves to the
utensil drawer. Whispers and sighs abound. Katherine
groans to Larry (she knows that addressing Joel is
useless), "This is beyond belief."

Larry turns his palms upward and shrugs.

The utensil drawer clatters as Joel tears it open.
He produces a sizeable carving knife. The blade's

teeth twinkle: a drooling smile. I see myself dying on the kitchen floor. Joel's breath is in my eyes: "You sure you wanna do this, son?"

"I'm the youngest one here," I say.

"What kind of answer is that? Just because you're able doesn't mean you're willing."

My mind is fogged. I can't tell the difference between willing and able. Where does one end and the other begin? I was willing to kill Paula's captors, but not fully able. I was able to help with Baby Selma's birth, but apparently unwilling. My shoulders tense up. This reminds me of Algebra class; too much noise in my head. "Cut me open right now," I say, my bare body quivering.

"First you gotta tell me you're sure," Joel grins.

"Why? So you don't feel guilty?"

"Yeah, something like that."

Have I ever been sure about anything? The only thing I know I'm sure of is that I want to see Selma. And I can't get to her if there are predators outside. *Desire* to see Selma . . . plus blood donation . . . equals *ability* to see Selma. Willingness begets ability in this case.

"Yes, I'm sure. Do it now."

"Where?"

"Right here in the kitchen," Larry deadpans. Nobody laughs.

"I don't know where," I breathe. "You're the one with the books."

"The books don't go into that," says Joel.

"Someplace fleshy," says Katherine.

Yeah, you'd like that, wouldn't you, Katherine? How 'bout I get out of these uncomfortable boxers?

"Your calf," Joel exhales. "What about your calf?"

I lift my foot off the floor and slam it on the tabletop, right above the clothes. Joel circles around me and grips my flesh. I laugh a little. (Now I know why Selma's legs were always ticklish.) Joel holds my calf with his left hand and aims the blade with his right. We make eye contact. I see no pleasure in him; he feels for me. And I feel for him feeling for me.

Until the metal teeth bite into my leg. Then I only feel pain.

I throw my head back and see a window in the ceiling. The glass reflects my blood spilling everywhere.

32.

Fifteen minutes later.

All lights are off. The senior citizens and myself stand before the kitchen window, which is open a crack. I've got a torn towel wrapped around my calf. Our bloody clothes are in the middle of the pool of gasoline out back. Nobody else seems to realize that the room is spinning.

We look and we wait.

"How long will this take?" Larry frowns.

"Will you stop with the complaining?" Joel moans.

Everybody stirs and shouts. Joel hisses, "*Ssshhh.*"

A horizontal silhouette saunters across the backyard. Nobody so much as blinks. Joel digs into his pocket and produces a box of wooden matches. He shakes open the box, picks out a match, takes aim, and stands ready to strike.

I can't help myself. "The second they catch fire," I whisper dizzily, "I have to run."

"Suit yourself," Larry nods, pumping my shoulder.

Another beast tiptoes across the yard. Both have manes. These may be my pals from the gas station. They circle around the soiled rags.

I think to myself, *That's right, motherfuckers. You're here to stay.*

Joel moves his match and matchbox toward the crack in the window.

"Let's go, let's go," somebody mutters.

I nod my head. Miraculously, it stays attached to my neck.

The animals study the clothing. They lick their chins and noses.

(When I was in grade school, we took a class trip to the zoo. There were hundreds of students on that trip, but only one thought between us: *We've gotta see the lions!* I never thought I'd relive the same emotion.)

Joel has a wheeze in his breath. Sounds like he has emphysema. Maybe that's why he's unafraid of the end; he's been preparing for it for a while. I place a hand on his back, behind his lungs. He says nothing, doesn't turn.

"There," whispers Larry.

A healthy female joins the two males. The animals examine the bait and make eye contact; the shoulder-free equivalent of shrugging.

"One more," Larry grins, more with wonderment than pleasure.

All eyes on the backyard.

I turn around and see a male lion standing in the hallway. His tongue hangs and drips. He seems unnaturally patient.

I blink to make the thought go away.

When I face the window again, I see pay dirt: four lions—two males, one female, and one bleeding, glassy mess—surrounding the precious threads. Their feet are planted in the grass. I pat myself on the back for being the owner of the blood.

Joel begins to strike the match, then pauses. "Wanna give us a little prayer, Kathy?"

Katherine squints and thinks before saying, "Dear Adonai: Help us light up these fucking bastards."

You got that, God?

Joel lights the match and tosses it out the window.

The lions' ears twitch.

A line of mystical orange snakes across the grass. When it hits the clothes, it changes from a line to a circle. The kitchen turns bright. The flames finger liquid from my pupils. I see the man in red race toward the flames (he must have been on the side of the house), then wave his arms wildly, spin around, and run away. No smile on his ugly face now. He leaves his whip to fry on the lawn.

The fat man grabs a water hose from the kitchen sink. Joel says, "Hang on a sec, Stan. Let them sizzle."

And sizzle they do. Aching cries explode from their upturned mouths. They run around the yard in fiery circles. Lights switch on in some neighbors' houses. I'm in desperate need of sunglasses.

One male's front legs collapse. Then a female's. They roll over on their backs and kick the air. The other male scrapes his side against a tree; the tree goes up in flames. Stan drags his hose toward the back door. Joel says, "Hang on. One's still standing."

The one that's still standing is the one that got hit by The Wolf. Some trooper she is. I admire her endurance. But I smile nonetheless when she drops.

Stan runs out the door. The lawn is covered with flames and blackened meat. I hear the fire hose's pressured hiss. I feel Joel's hands on my shoulders. He whispers in my ear, "You're an angel."

I turn to him. His blue eyes reflect the flames.

I press my forehead against Joel's and shut my eyes. Maybe a little of his essence will pass into me.

Joel pats the small of my back as I slip past him.

I head toward the front door. Seniors line the hallway, all of them staring and nodding. I suppose that I could walk to Selma's house, but I don't really feel like it.

It would be much more appropriate to run.

33.

Selma's family is huddled in the bay window. They're little black smudges from where I stand. If I had more time, I would pause for a breath, but I need every moment I can get. Plus, I'm in no mood to encounter my friend with the red jacket. With any luck, he's curled up under a tree somewhere, crying his way toward death.

I want Selma to open the door, run across the lawn to me, and smother me with her mouth, but she's afraid of the lions, so I have to go up to the porch.

I knock only once. No locks turning or chains jingling—the door opens right away. If there's a prettier girl on Earth, I haven't met her. Selma's face is pale with anxiety and exhaustion, but it punches me in the chest and nearly knocks me down. Her lips—

always so smooth that, when my eyes were closed, I could never tell where they ended and where her cheeks and chin began—are on me, kissing my eyelids and forehead and cheeks and wounds.

She tells me I took forever. I tell her not to say words like *forever*. She warns me to step inside before I get attacked by a lion. I tell her it's too late, and not to worry about lions from now on. Then I say to her, weakly, not to worry about anything anymore, because I'm here and she's here and we love each other and nothing else matters. She touches my elbow and leads me into her chilly foyer. This is the last time I will step indoors. Before I know it, I am at Selma's kitchen table, drinking cranberry juice. Selma's father is forcing a smile and asking me what it was like out there. I tell him, "It was grand," and sip my juice.

The plan is to die in the living room, on the carpet, in a collapsed huddle, down on our knees, cheeks pressed together, palms touching backs. Well, they don't go into that much detail, but that's what I envision. I say that that's a good idea, and through deep breaths I politely (as politely as possible) say to Selma's parents that I know every minute counts but I would still—if it's no problem—like to talk to Selma alone for just a moment.

In actuality, the moment is seventeen min-utes—seventeen long minutes that fortunately feel like thirty—wherein I hold Selma in the shower of the upstairs bathroom. I touch her wet upper back and think of my mother, and wonder for a moment if my mother called Selma's parents to see if I made it here okay, but I know that Mom's too much of a realist for such a move. I wonder if they miss me right now, my awesome family, but I don't have to wonder about that either, because I'm sure that they do. (And also, somewhere deeper, I'm sure that they'll be fine.)

Selma cries into the crook of my shoulder; her tears aren't theatrical or mannered like they were back during some of our fights; they're soft and slow and from somewhere deep; full of regret; oh, what we might have done if only we had had more time.

It's like a funeral with beating hearts in the coffins. I enter Selma's body briefly—too briefly, but long enough to feel that tender friction that makes me her and her me and us us—and she hisses through closed teeth and throws her head back; she's not wet enough, but she wants me inside her so bad that she's willing to go through pain. Just like I wanted to see her so bad that I was willing to go through hell.

I don't know if we would have made it had we lived longer. Objectively speaking, she's a little too loose and I'm a little too tightly wound, but maybe in the long run that would have made for vital chemistry. In any case, there's no more long run. We're cruising down the short run, and we're the best each other can find.

When Selma's eyelashes are wet, she looks like a mystical creature come from exotic lands, a mermaid or a sensual alien. Beads of water use her top lashes as hammocks; the lower ones droop and reveal to me her powerful eyes. She doesn't look at me, she looks into me, as if there's something in here, something soulful and true. By now, I should know whether or not I think the same. But I don't, and I may not ever. The sublimity I witnessed after Baby Selma's birth has slipped back into the woodwork, but that doesn't mean I don't sense an afterlife. Who says divinity must glow? Maybe it's plain; maybe God is plain. For all we know, this whole paradise business is as banal as your corner grocer. No trumpets play when you arrive. You just get winks and nods from the established patrons, some of whom chuckle and say to you, "What? You were expecting a welcoming committee?"

And that would be okay. Anything would be nicer than nothingness. Except for hell, of course. But I don't really buy into that shit. Something kind of melodramatic about the thought of red demons flashing their teeth. Besides, like I said, I've seen hell already, and as far as I'm concerned it's quite beatable.

Selma stands in front of me. I towel her off: chest, belly, pubis. Till the very end, she never stopped shaving. (Perhaps she shaved after our morning phone call.) I'd like to chew gently on her for hours. Her nipple resting on my tongue would amply constitute paradise. We hug each other; bare flesh, her soft chest against my hard one, my hard waist against her soft one. The two of us.

"We have to go downstairs," she says. Every word like mist. Even the consonants are soft. I don't want to nod, but I do. She touches my hand. Time to go downstairs and meet The Man Upstairs. Or Woman, as the case may be.

We run. Selma in front of me; her legs, her shoulders, her back. I want to kiss the part in her hair.

I don't know if I'm whole; I may not be. I've done my best. But I know my love is whole. As I put one arm around Selma and another around her mother, with her father's forehead against mine, I feel a love so ferocious it belongs in a cage. I am sure that this feeling will last. As for everything else?

It's only temporary.

ABOUT THE AUTHOR

Eric Shapiro's wide array of fiction and nonfiction pieces have appeared in over 75 publications, in print and on the World Wide Web, including *The Elastic Book of Numbers* (Elastic Press) and *Fedora IV* (Betancourt & Co.).

Eric's debut, *Short of a Picnic* (2002), a radical fiction collection about mental illness, enjoyed critical and commercial success, and his screenplay *Male Revenge Fantasy* received a national award from the International Radio & Television Society in 1998.

Eric lives in Los Angeles with his wife Rhoda. He will not be satisfied with his fiction until the pages literally catch fire . . .

D.L. SNELL

Hourglass

A single father braves dank mines, train tunnels and carnivorous forests, in search of the last hourglass tree, the only hope of saving his son from the deadly sting of an arachnid wasp.

"Tightens like a noose."
~C.D. Phillips, editor, *eye-rhyme*

Exit66.net/indexbooks.htm

Anthology Appearances

- **Cold Flesh,** Hellbound Books
- **The Undead,** Permuted Press
- **Monsters Ink,** Cyber Pulp
- **Mind Scraps,** Cyber Pulp

Ghostwriter

An evil priest sicks his congregation on a best-selling novelist, who relies on an un-identified entity to write his books.

"Frightful. I couldn't put it down."
~Nora Weston, author of @hell

Exit66.net/indexbooks.htm

THE UNDEAD

A ZOMBIE ANTHOLOGY
CONTAINING SHORT HORRORS BY
VINCE CHURCHILL, D.L. SNELL,
ERIC S. BROWN, AND MANY MORE.

Afterword by Brian Keene

Foreword by Kevin Sproles

COMING LATE 2005

PermutedPress.com

Aliens... Angels...
Demons... Zombies...
Ancient Evils...
Modern Horrors...
These are

MADMEN'S DREAMS

Eric S. Brown and D. Richard Pearce present a deranged collection of horror and sci-fi tales so startling they could only come from the nightmares of the insane.

"Eric S. Brown is...a whirlwind of talent, dedication, and good old fashioned scares."—Brian Keene, author of *The Rising*

"Brown is well on his way to making a name for himself in dark fiction."—Scott Nicholson, author of *The Manor*

Out Now! Order at PermutedPress.com, most online bookstores, or ask your local retailer.

ISBN: 0-9765559-1-3